LIVE
LIKE A
GODDESS

Crocodile Books, USA
An imprint of Interlink Publishing Group, Inc.
www.interlinkbooks.com

For all the women who raised me.

First American edition published in 2024 by

Crocodile Books
An imprint of Interlink Publishing Group, Inc.
46 Crosby Street
Northampton, Massachusetts 01060
www.interlinkbooks.com

Text copyright © Jean Menzies 2023
Illustration copyright © Taylor Dolan 2023

First published in Great Britain in 2023 by Wren & Rook, An imprint of
Hachette Children's Group, London

Library of Congress Cataloging-in-Publication Data available
ISBN 978-1-62371-657-8

2 4 6 8 10 9 7 5 3 1

Printed and bound in Korea

JEAN MENZIES

ILLUSTRATED BY TAYLOR DOLAN

LIVE LIKE A GODDESS

LIFE LESSONS FROM LEGENDS AND LORE

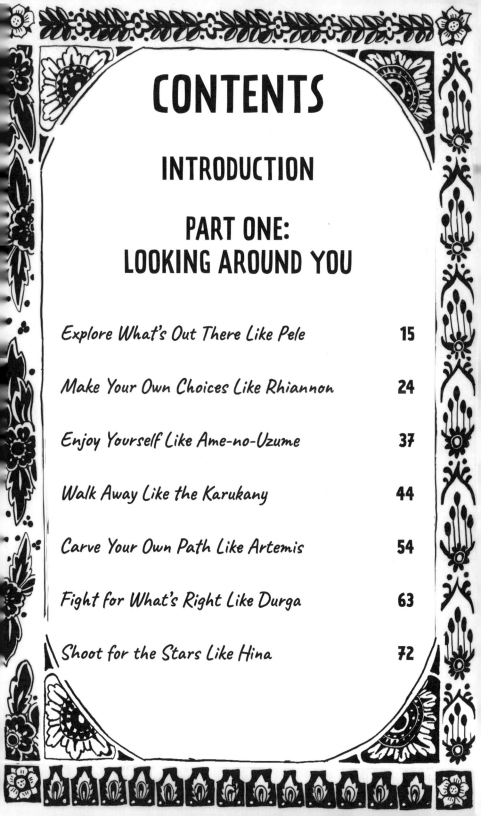

CONTENTS

INTRODUCTION

PART ONE:
LOOKING AROUND YOU

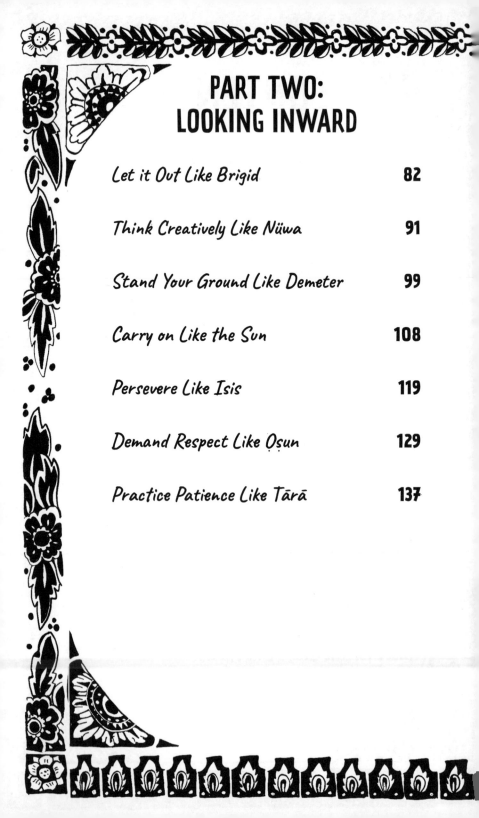

PART TWO:
LOOKING INWARD

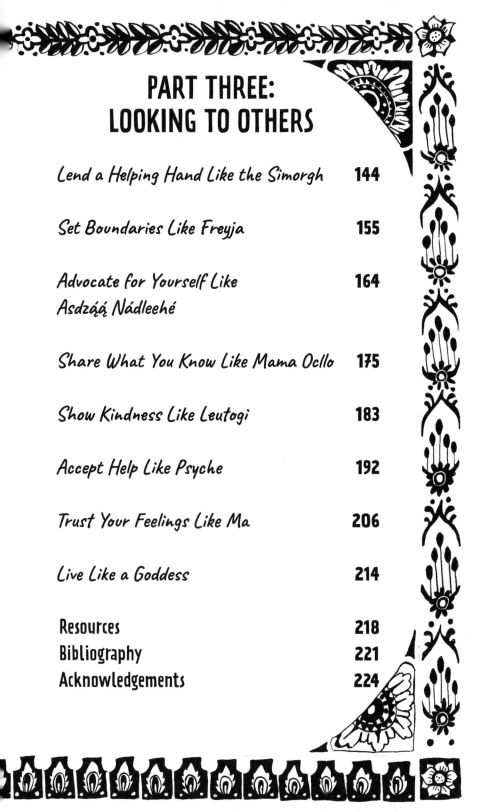

PART THREE: LOOKING TO OTHERS

INTRODUCTION

I don't know about you, but when I'm struggling to make sense of my emotions or I'm faced with a decision I've never had to make before, it can feel like an incredibly lonely experience. The thing is, as unique as each of our own journeys are, people have had to learn to navigate new and sometimes difficult situations since the dawn of time—and not just mere mortals like us. Countless cultures and religions across the world celebrate goddesses who have faced challenges big and small, from how to cheer up a friend all the way to how to rebuild the universe itself.

These goddesses and mythical women are some of the strongest and most powerful beings ever imagined, but like us, they had their own obstacles to overcome. Rather than having it all sorted from the get-go, these women encountered their fair share of sadness and confusion, bullying and sexism, unexpected challenges and big decisions—not unlike what many of us still tackle today. Unsurprisingly, therefore, these legendary ladies have a lot to teach us, from handling difficult situations to embracing happiness. And I can't wait to introduce (or reintroduce) them and their myths to you. Before we jump in, I think it's important to establish what exactly a myth is.

The word myth comes from the ancient Greek word *mythos*, which simply means story.

And that's exactly what this book contains. Stories from different cultures, people and religions. Stories that have been told for centuries or even millennia. Stories that are spoken aloud over meals or written down in books for others to read. Stories that contain truths about the world and human experiences in their endless variety. And each woman's myth holds a great amount of meaning to those who celebrate their legacy. But these meanings can vary and transform. The same myth might mean one thing one century and another the next. Its significance can change depending on time, place, narrator or reader.

The ancient Greek playwright Euripides, for example, took a well-known myth that celebrated wartime victory and retold it to explore the tragic consequences of conflict in *Trojan Women*.

While the story and characters remained the same, they meant something different to Euripides than they had to someone else, but neither interpretation was right or wrong. So while I've shared what these goddesses' stories mean to me, don't be afraid to find your own meaning and inspiration in their incredible tales.

The brave and clever women you'll meet in this book have been and continue to be beacons of hope, lessons in tragedy and fountains of wisdom for countless people around the world. And this book is a moment to celebrate their stories again, for you to interpret and learn from them in a way that helps you on your own path. So I hope that by reading these empowering women's stories, you too can learn something about how to navigate your journey through life and be just as **fierce** in your future. Whether you are inspired by the kindness of Leutogi or the courage of the Sun, the ingenuity of Nüwa or the confidence of Freyja, remember that you too can live like a goddess (whether you're a supreme immortal being or not).

PART ONE

LOOKING AROUND YOU

EXPLORE WHAT'S OUT THERE LIKE PELE

Feeling stuck in a rut or just desperate to try something new? Find inspiration from Pele's own adventure.

WHO IS PELE?

Pele is the Hawaiian goddess of volcanoes and fire. She is the daughter of the mother goddess Haumea and, depending on which version of her story you read, the sky god Kāne-milo-hai or the sea god Kū-waha-ilo. Pele is also believed to have founded the early civilizations of the Hawaiian Islands, which explains why Hawai'i has more volcanoes than anywhere else. Today she is still said to live in Kīlauea, the most active of Hawai'i's five volcanoes. Pele is an unpredictable deity who either causes eruptions or warns humans of their impending danger, depending on her mood.

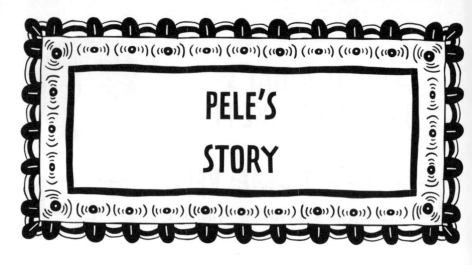

PELE'S STORY

The young goddess Pele lived alongside her mother, Haumea, and father, Kū-waha-ilo. Although she loved her parents dearly, as the years passed, she could not help but grow curious about the world beyond their home. She spent her days dreaming of far-off lands and imagining the places she may one day go. Finally, her desire to explore grew too large to be contained and she approached Kū-waha-ilo with her plans.

"Father, will you give me a boat so that I might travel the seas and discover what else exists out there?" Pele asked.

"I would consider your request, but what of your little sister's egg? After all, you made a promise to care for it until her birth," Kū-waha-ilo replied, nodding at a large egg in which the unborn goddess Hi'aka slept.

16

Pele had already considered this, and she lifted the egg in her arms, wrapping it in her long skirts so that it lay warm and safe against her body.

"Don't worry, Father, I will keep her with me until the time comes for her egg to hatch."

Finding no other reason to object, Kū-waha-ilo conceded to his daughter's request.

"Go to your brother Kamohoali'i and on my instructions, he will build you the boat you desire."

So, Pele did just that. Eagerly, she watched as Kamohoali'i assembled a canoe with strong sails made from matted palm leaves, large enough to hold food for many weeks.

While she waited, her brother asked her where she would go. But Pele could not provide a single answer because she planned on going everywhere. Finally, when the canoe was complete, the young goddess bid farewell to her family and boarded her vessel, ready to set sail.

First, Pele navigated her ship through the Society Islands, beginning with Bora Bora. Next, she visited the ancestral islands of Kuai-he-lanai, Kane-huna-moku and Mokumanamana.

Along the way, she met Queen Kaoahi of Ni'ihau and passed a few happy days with friendly conversation. When Pele landed on the island of Kaua'i, she marveled at the sprawling gardens and magnificent array of plants that sprouted from the rich volcanic soil, many of which she had never encountered before. This place, she thought, would make a beautiful home.

Along with her other supplies, Pele had brought with her a magical wooden staff known as Pa'ao. The staff served as a useful digging tool, and so she struck the earth of Kaua'i hoping to carve a home for herself. When she dug down

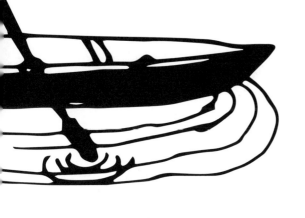

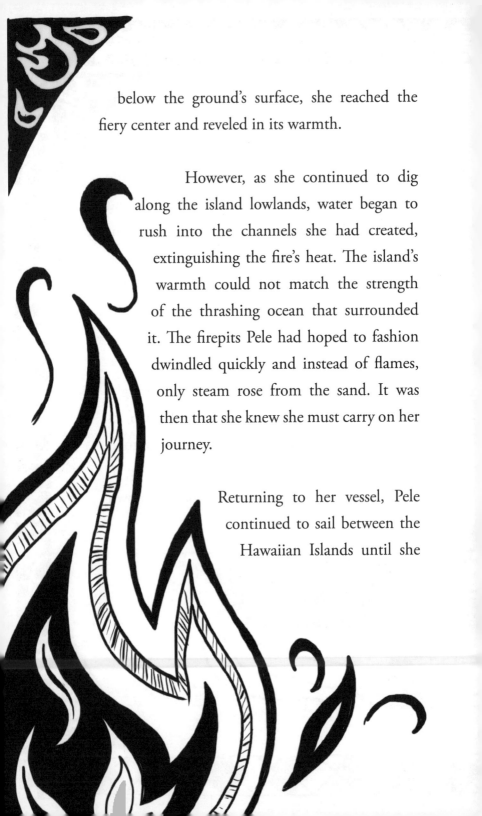

below the ground's surface, she reached the fiery center and reveled in its warmth.

However, as she continued to dig along the island lowlands, water began to rush into the channels she had created, extinguishing the fire's heat. The island's warmth could not match the strength of the thrashing ocean that surrounded it. The firepits Pele had hoped to fashion dwindled quickly and instead of flames, only steam rose from the sand. It was then that she knew she must carry on her journey.

Returning to her vessel, Pele continued to sail between the Hawaiian Islands until she reached the island of Hawai'i itself. This island was the largest of the archipelago and home to a ferocious volcano known as Kīlauea, which is still active today.

Once again, Pele used Pa'ao to dig deep down into the core of the mountainside and release the fire within. Although the ocean tried to quell the heat she released, the strength of Kīlauea was too great. That was when Pele knew she had found what she had been looking for. And so, it seemed, did her little sister, for it was here that Hi'aka's egg hatched, joining Pele in their new home. Slowly but surely, Pele built a splendid palace of fire on the island as her home, while Hi'aka settled in a grove of lehua trees. Finally, when Pele was satisfied with her work, she invited the rest of their brothers and sisters to join them in the beautiful home she had found thanks to her adventure.

BE MORE LIKE PELE

The world has more to offer than it is possible to imagine. You don't even have to sail far from home to discover what is out there. Embracing your sense of adventure or curiosity, like Pele did, could mean visiting a new city or traveling abroad, but it could also mean experimenting with a new hobby or visiting a local attraction you've never been to before.

It is perfectly possible to expand your own world from your own bubble. Join a book club, and you might meet new people. Sign up to an online course, and you could discover an untapped passion. Volunteer with a local organization, and you might find a new purpose. You don't have to go far to eat new food, try new things or marvel at the beauty of nature.

You might learn of even more places you'd like to go, or simply return home with a new appreciation of where you came from and full of stories about what you've seen. Just remember to prepare ahead like Pele did, whether you need a canoe or just your trusty backpack.

MAKE YOUR OWN CHOICES LIKE RHIANNON

 —— **NAME: RHIANNON** ——

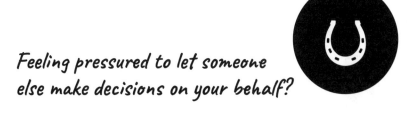

Feeling pressured to let someone else make decisions on your behalf?

Learn from Rhiannon's independent choices.

WHO IS RHIANNON?

Rhiannon is a noblewoman of the Otherworld, whose people are sometimes known as fairies in Welsh mythology. Her name means "divine queen" in Welsh and may derive from an earlier British deity known as Rigantona in Brittonic.

She is also sometimes identified as the Celtic goddess of horses, an affinity she later passes on to her son Pryderi, who is fathered by the hero Pwyll. When Pryderi is abducted on the night of his birth, Rhiannon's lady's maids frame her for killing the baby to avoid blame, but Pwyll refuses to believe the rumors or cast Rhiannon aside. Eventually, they are reunited with their child, and Pwyll is proven right in trusting his wife.

RHIANNON'S STORY

There once existed a sacred mound, and it was said that if a man should sit atop, he would see either something terrible or something wonderful. Never one to back down from a challenge, Pwyll, lord of the Welsh county Dyfed, decided to take a seat upon the mound. As he sat there, he watched and waited, curious about what he would see. It was at this time that the fair lady Rhiannon passed by astride a horse as white as freshly fallen snow.

Pwyll was taken aback by the strange woman's beauty and immediately commanded his nearest guard to hail her down. The man rode his own horse in the woman's direction, but she did not stop for him. No matter how fast he pushed his steed, he could not catch up. The ghostly maiden remained just out of reach. Eventually, the guard gave up and returned to his lord, defeated.

"No matter." Pwyll smiled kindly. "We will simply have to return tomorrow."

And so they did. Just as before, Pwyll sat upon the mound waiting for the lady Rhiannon to appear in the distance. This time, he sent his fastest rider to flag her down, but once again the rider could not catch up to her.

On the third day, Pwyll decided to take matters into his own hands, and when the beautiful woman appeared, he mounted his own horse and began to chase after her. However, just like his men, Pwyll could not reach her, no matter how fast he rode. Finally, he pulled his horse to a stop and cried out to the woman instead.

"My lady, won't you wait for me?"

At these words, Rhiannon slowed her gallop and turned to face the lord.

"Why didn't you say so sooner?" She laughed. "All you had to do was ask."

After that, they rode together for a little while, talking animatedly about their lives.

"What brings you here, Rhiannon?" Pwyll eventually asked.

"I must confess," she said, grinning sheepishly, "you do. I saw you on your first day here and could not get you out of my mind. My father meanwhile has betrothed me to another, a man I care nothing for. So I came again to ask if you would be my husband instead?"

"My lady," Pwyll replied, "if I could choose from every woman in this world and the next, it would be you I chose."

After that a date was set, a year from then, when they would reunite as husband and wife. The twelve months passed, then an extravagant

feast was prepared, and Rhiannon and Pwyll took their seats beside each other, ready to bind themselves to one another for eternity. But before their marriage could take place, their celebrations were interrupted by an unexpected guest. The man, who Pwyll had never seen before, presented himself to the bride and groom.

"Lord Pwyll of Dyfed, I have come to ask of you a favor."

"Anything!" Pwyll declared, overflowing with merriment and joy. Rhiannon, however, let out a gasp and her expression fell.

"Pwyll, what have you done?" she groaned.

"I don't understand." Pwyll furrowed his brow.

"This is Gwawl, son of Cud, the man my father would have me marry."

"I am," added Gwawl. "And I have come to ask for Rhiannon as my wife once more."

Pwyll was horrified at what he had done. He was bound by his word to grant this man whatever favor he requested, but Gwawl had asked for the one thing Pwyll could not bear to give. Rhiannon, meanwhile, was not about to allow two men to trade her between them, no matter how she might love Pwyll. She would simply have to solve Pwyll's conundrum for him.

First, she told Gwawl to return in one year's time, and on that date they would hold their own wedding feast. Then, when Gwawl was gone, she turned to Pwyll and handed him a tattered sack.

"When my wedding with Gwawl is underway, you must arrive dressed in ragged clothes and ask him if you might fill your sack with food from the feast. I have placed a spell upon the bag that means no matter how much you place inside there will always be room for more. Eventually, Gwawl will ask when your sack will be full. Tell him only when a man of noble birth steps inside to flatten the contents with his feet. Gwawl will surely volunteer, and when he does, you must pull the cloth up over his head and tie it closed. He will not be able to escape on his own."

Pwyll took the sack from his beloved, and when twelve months had passed, he arrived at the wedding of Gwawl and Rhiannon, bag in hand.

"What brings you here, my man?" asked Gwawl.

"Will you allow me to fill my sack with food from your tables, my lord?"

Gwawl thought this a reasonable request and nodded for Pwyll to proceed. Yet, just as Rhiannon had said, the sack never grew full. Finally, when their guest had almost cleared the tables, Gwawl called out for Pwyll to stop, demanding to know what was going on. Pwyll explained that the sack would never be full until a man of noble birth steps inside to flatten the contents. Gwawl rose from his seat, took the sack from Pwyll, placed one foot inside, then the other, and began to stomp his boots down on the food. Pwyll moved swiftly and pulled the strings of the bag up until Gwawl's head was covered. He tied them tightly over the man and then proceeded to spin the bag in circles above his head, smiling all the while.

"Let me out!" cried Gwawl.

"First make me a deal," came the voice of Rhiannon, who had been watching all the while. "Pwyll will free you only if you free me first. Relinquish my hand in marriage, and you will be allowed to walk away from here unscathed."

"Fine, fine, just get me out!"

Happily, Pwyll did just that, sending Gwawl on his way and taking Rhiannon in his arms once more.

"Since our first wedding was so rudely interrupted, I think it might be time to finally exchange our vows, don't you?" the lady laughed, giving him a kiss hello.

And so they wed that very night, both having chosen each other as their own.

BE MORE LIKE RHIANNON

Remember, your choices are yours to make and yours alone. You may find that people will offer you advice, whether they are someone you trust or an expert with information that could help you understand your decision better. But, when it comes down to it, you should never feel pressured to do anything you don't want to do simply because someone else wants you to. You don't have to be with someone you don't want to be with, you don't have to go somewhere that makes you uncomfortable and you don't have to take a path in life that will make you unhappy.

Rhiannon knew this. She chose Pwyll and fought for the happiness she deserved, even when it might have seemed easier just to marry Gwawl in the face of Pwyll's mistake. So, like Rhiannon, choose the people and places that make you smile, and don't let any potential hurdles stop you from being your authentic self.

ENJOY YOURSELF LIKE AME-NO-UZUME

┌─ **NAME:** 天鈿女命 (JAPANESE KANJI) ─┐
ALSO KNOWN AS AME-NO-UZUME OR
└─ **AME-NO-UZUME-NO-MIKOTO** ─┘

Don't take life too seriously. Dance your way through it like Ame-no-Uzume!

WHO IS AME-NO-UZUME?

Ame-no-Uzume is the Shinto goddess of the dawn, dance and merriment. Shinto is a widespread polytheistic religion (a religion which involves worshipping more than one god) throughout Japan, which celebrates divine spirits known as Kami. A number of modern-day Shinto shrines are dedicated to Ame-no-Uzume across Japan. The goddess is also said to have married the Shinto god Sarutahiko Ōkami. Together, they founded the historical Sarume clan of Japan, who served the royal court as dancers and performers.

AME-NO-UZUME'S STORY

An unending darkness had fallen across the heavens, and it was all because of Susanowo, mischievous god of the sea and storms. For Susanowo had come to live with the goddess of the sun, known as Amaterasu, but rather than behave himself as a guest would be expected to, he had plagued the goddess night and day. The final straw came when, on the day Amaterasu was to celebrate the feast of first fruits, Susanowo decided to relieve himself throughout her palace as a nasty joke! Furious, Amaterasu retreated to her cave, sealing the stone door behind her. Without her presence, the sun no longer rose each morning, and so the other gods and goddesses debated what to do.

At first, they stood outside the cave, pleading with the goddess and making offerings to tempt her out. When none of their offerings enticed her, the goddess Ame-no-Uzume came up with a plan. Now, Ame-no-Uzume was an expert in all things pleasurable, and she knew the power of joy in the face of rage.

First, she plucked the leaves and branches from the heavenly sakaki tree and fashioned a headdress for herself. Next, she gathered lengths of thick clubmoss and braided a sash to tie around her waist. With the sash in place, she was able to tuck away the long sleeves of her kimono to free her arms for what came next.

Ame-no-Uzume lit the nearby brazier heaters so that their flames flickered and cast a pleasant glow upon the space. She then flipped an enormous tub and climbed atop it so she could be observed from all sides. With her stage set, Ame-no-Uzume began to dance. Her movements were bold and graceful, her arms creating mesmerizing shapes as they passed through the air. The other gods and goddesses were entranced, and one by one, they began to clap and cheer. What a sight to behold, they thought, momentarily distracted from the sun's troubling absence.

When her performance was in full swing, Ame-no-Uzume finally launched into song, chanting loudly above the now uproarious sound of the other deities' delight. All this noise penetrated Amaterasu's cave. The sun goddess was shocked at what she heard. How can they be so jolly when I have cast them into eternal night, she thought.

Finally, her curiosity grew too strong, and she began to push the rock-cave's entrance aside. Noticing the movement, the gathered crowd

turned their heads, and the gods Nakatomi and Imibe rushed forward to greet the goddess before she could change her mind.

"Stay, Amaterasu," they begged, gesturing to Ame-no-Uzume, who smiled down from atop her tub. "Join us in our revelry, and we will promise to punish Susanowo for his rudeness once we are done."

Feeling better, Amaterasu nodded her assent, and as she looked up at Ame-no-Uzume's display, a small smiled stretched across her lips. Ame-no-Uzume's joy was infectious, it seemed.

BE MORE LIKE AME-NO-UZUME

OK, so I'm not suggesting that inviting your friends over for karaoke or sitting down to watch your favorite film is going to save the world, but that doesn't mean you should underestimate the power of joy. Life is for living, after all. Join a dance class, learn that musical instrument or play that video game. Visit your favorite coffee shop, read that fantasy book or invite someone over to play a board game or two.

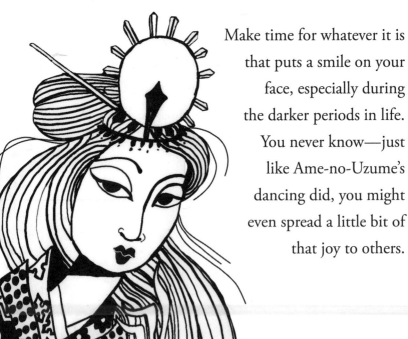

Make time for whatever it is that puts a smile on your face, especially during the darker periods in life. You never know—just like Ame-no-Uzume's dancing did, you might even spread a little bit of that joy to others.

WALK AWAY LIKE THE KARUKANY

44

Do you feel trapped in a toxic relationship or situation?

The Karukany reminds us it's never too late to take the first step towards a better life.

WHO IS THE KARUKANY?

The Karukany is a figure from the legends of the Gurindji, an Indigenous people based in northern Australia. Similarly to European mermaids, the Karukany has a human body from the waist up while her lower half is the tail of a fish. Yet, unlike many merfolk, the Karukany's tail can be removed to reveal human legs beneath. Her story is typically told from the perspective of the fisherman who captures the Karukany and whose arrogance loses him what he desires but does not deserve. It may even be intended as a warning that otherworldly creatures do not belong in the human world. But the Karukany's story is her own, and so I think it's high time we consider it from her perspective.

THE KARUKANY'S STORY

That day, just like any other, the Karukany and her friend lay warming themselves on the rocks. Together, they had swum up from their underwater home to lounge with the crocodiles on the shore and enjoy the midday sun. So relaxed were they that neither of them noticed the man watching them from a distance. He was a local fisherman, and he had spied the two women earlier that week, only to return three days later with a wicked plan.

The fisherman covered his head with thick bundles of river grass bound together by mud from the water's edge. The blades of grass were so long that once he had finished applying them, they covered nearly every inch of his body. When his disguise was complete, the man lowered himself into the river and began to slowly swim in the direction of the Karukany and her friend. From an outsider's perspective he appeared as nothing more than a lump of grass being swept along by the water.

It was not until the fisherman was almost upon them that the Karukany realized what was happening. Her friend screamed and jumped into the water, but before the Karukany could follow, the man had his arms around her. She fought with all her strength, but his grip was too tight. Ignoring her cries for help, her captor dragged her far from the riverbank until they reached a small firepit with smoke rising out of it in thick tendrils.

To the Karukany's horror, the fisherman bound her and held her over the pit so that the smoke penetrated her skin and scales. Slowly but surely, the hot flames cracked her scales, and the Karukany felt her beloved tail begin to loosen and fall away. Finally, after what felt like an age, the fisherman lifted her from the pit to reveal two human legs where her fish tail had once been. Defeated, the Karukany did not struggle when he untied her wrists and took her hand. She simply accepted his iron grip and followed him to the camp where he spent his nights.

From that day on, the Karukany rarely left the fisherman's side. He took her wherever he went and told whomever he met that they were husband and wife. There was one exception to this routine, however; never did the Karukany see the river again. When the fisherman went out to work, he left her at home, and she passed the hours alone and confused, slowly forgetting the home she had been forced to leave.

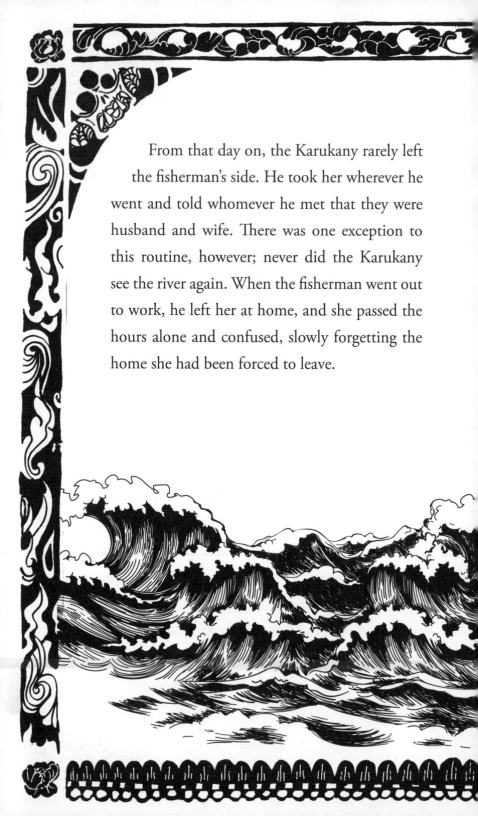

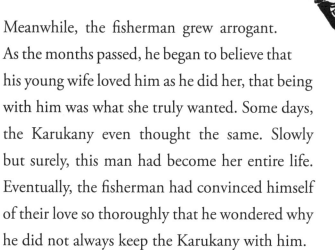

Meanwhile, the fisherman grew arrogant. As the months passed, he began to believe that his young wife loved him as he did her, that being with him was what she truly wanted. Some days, the Karukany even thought the same. Slowly but surely, this man had become her entire life. Eventually, the fisherman had convinced himself of their love so thoroughly that he wondered why he did not always keep the Karukany with him.

So it was that the next time the man went fishing in the river, he brought his wife along.

The man and woman set up camp by the side of the river. When the working day was done, they sat down to cook themselves a meal. As she ate, the Karukany stared into the rippling water illuminated by the light of the moon. It seemed so familiar, this place, she mused, like somewhere she had been before. Peering deeper into the river, she felt a pang inside her heart. For so long, she had experienced only numbness there, but in that moment, she realized something had changed. Here, she thought, is my home.

When her husband stood to stretch his legs, the Karukany told him she would wait by their camp, too tired to walk with him that night. The fisherman shrugged and set off on foot along the shore, humming to himself all the while. The Karukany watched patiently as he wandered further and further away.

Finally, when the man's figure appeared no bigger than her little finger in the distance, she rose to her feet and ran. One foot in front of the other, the Karukany sprinted in the direction of the river as fast as she could. When her toes finally touched the water, she transformed. The human legs she had lived with for so long grew scales and her feet stretched beyond recognition.

Within mere seconds of submerging herself in the river, the Karukany felt her tail return entirely. What once had been so cruelly taken from her, she had reclaimed. Then, without a second thought for the fisherman, the Karukany dove beneath the water, never to be seen again.

BE MORE LIKE THE KARUKANY

In her story, the Karukany is taken from her home, isolated from her loved ones and made to rely solely on one person. She is treated cruelly and selfishly by someone who claims to love her, and escape seems impossible. But the Karukany does escape. She is reminded that she existed before her partner, that she is her own person and that her life belongs to her alone.

That's not to say what she did was easy or that she did not doubt herself, but the Karukany recognized that her relationship wasn't healthy or making her happy, and she took the first step in leaving it behind.

While it might seem obvious to an outsider that the Karukany was in a toxic situation, sometimes an unhealthy relationship is more difficult to recognize when it's happening to you. But it's never too late to walk away from the thing or person holding you back.

If the Karukany's situation does feel familiar to you or someone you know, please take a look at the resources at the back of this book.

CARVE YOUR OWN PATH LIKE ARTEMIS

NAME: Άρτεμις (GREEK ALPHABET)

ALSO KNOWN AS ARTEMIS, PHÔSPHOROS OR PHOEBE

Trying to figure out which path to take?

Maybe Artemis's story can help inspire your journey.

WHO IS ARTEMIS?

Artemis is the ancient Greek goddess of the hunt. In addition to this role, she is also an important goddess of childbirth and midwifery in ancient Greece. She is the daughter of the god Zeus and the goddess Leto, as well as the twin sister of Apollo, god of music. She is a skilled archer and generally spends her days out hunting with her dogs or relaxing with her handmaids, as opposed to spending time on Mount Olympus with the other deities. Along with Athena and Hestia, she is also one of the three maiden goddesses in ancient Greek mythology.

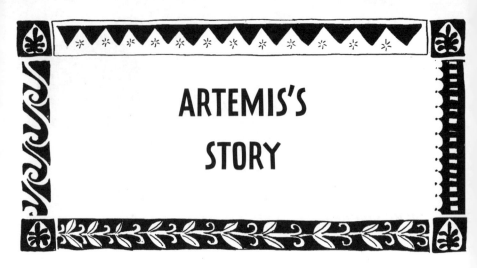

ARTEMIS'S STORY

From the day she was born, Artemis was already capable beyond her years. Her mother, Leto, did not have an easy labor. Hated by Zeus' wife, Hera, for becoming pregnant with his children, Leto was forced to roam the land alone until she found sanctuary on the Isle of Delos. There, she gave birth to her daughter Artemis with little trouble, but her second child, the girl's twin, was not so easy. So it was that Artemis herself had to assist in her brother Apollo's birth!

Artemis was so calm and independent the first day she walked the earth, it was clear that she would carve a path of her own. When the goddess was a little older, but still not fully grown, Artemis sat on her father Zeus' knee and asked if, as his daughter, he would allow her ten requests.

"Go on, tell me what it is you would like," said the god, grinning down at the bold little girl on his lap.

"First, I would like to never marry or take a lover. I have no interests in romance or desire as Aphrodite puts it."

"Go on." Zeus nodded.

"I wish to have as many names as my brother so we can always be told apart. And most of all, I wish to be referred to as bringer of light. I would also like a bow with arrows and an embroidered tunic short enough to hunt."

"You don't want much, I see." Zeus laughed, but Artemis continued.

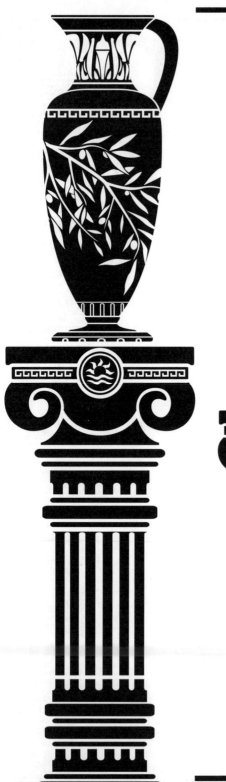

"Grant me sixty of Oceanus's daughters, nymphs all nine years old, to be my choir, and twenty Amnisiades nymphs as my handmaids to tend my dogs when not out hunting. Give me domain over all the mountains and whichever city you should chose. But allow me to visit the homes of men only when a woman calls for my help in childbirth, so that I might ease her pain as I did my mother, Leto."

"Are you done, little one?" Zeus asked Artemis, who simply nodded. "Well, you shall have all those things and more. You shall have thirty cities, not just one. Thirty cities that will worship Artemis above any other god on Olympus."

And with that Artemis was off; there were bows and arrows to be made, and handmaids to choose after all.

BE MORE LIKE ARTEMIS

Don't be afraid to walk the untrodden path. Sometimes life means doing what's right for you as opposed to what's expected of you, when those two things do not align. There may be pressure from loved ones or the outside world to follow a certain path—there may even be a small voice inside your head telling you that this is what your future must be—but just because it's what has been done before doesn't mean it's what you must do. Remember, there is a first time for everything.

Like Artemis, you might choose to eschew romantic love or pursue a career no one expected you to follow. This is your life, your time on planet Earth, your chance to find the road most suitable for you—even if it's the one less traveled.

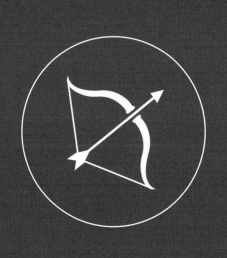

FIGHT FOR WHAT'S RIGHT LIKE DURGA

*Want to see real change in the world around you?
Be inspired to be part of that change by Durga's story.*

WHO IS DURGA?

Durga is a Hindu goddess of war and motherhood. She is deemed the protector of the universe from all evil, first coming to life to slay the buffalo demon Mahishasura. The annual ten-day festival of Durga Puja is held during the Hindu calendar month of Ashvin and celebrates both the goddess and her defeat of Mahishasura. Durga is often depicted in art riding a lion or tiger into battle, carrying various weapons in her many hands. In these images, she has anywhere between four and eighteen arms, while certain texts describe her as possessing at least a thousand.

DURGA'S STORY

Long ago, a war raged between the gods. On one side was Indra, king of the gods, while on the other was the buffalo demon Mahishasura and his followers, power-hungry beings known as asuras. Although Indra and the other gods fought valiantly, Mahishasura had once been granted a rare and coveted gift that gave him the upper hand: he could not die at the hands of another man. Finally, after four hundred years of fighting had passed, Mahishasura was victorious, and to the horror of the gods and goddesses, he ousted Indra from his throne.

While the asuras rained cruelty down on humankind, the deities who had fought with Indra were thrown from the heavens and forced to live on earth as though they were mortals. Desperate to regain the heavens, they discussed what should be done. It was Brahma, god of creation, who suggested they approach the gods Vishnu and Shiva for the answer. So all thirty gods, Indra and Brahma included, brought their tale to Vishnu and Shiva.

Vishnu and Shiva exchanged a look, sure of what must be done. They brought their hands together and let loose a dazzling light formed of their fury. This light grew and morphed until it almost resembled the shape of another person. Then, one by one, lights spewed forth from each of the gathered gods in turn and joined the mysterious form. Shiva's light gave the figure a face, while Yama, god of death, provided light for its hair. Vishnu's brilliance formed its arms, while Varuna, god of the waters, contributed its legs. Finally, when the body was complete, the gathered deities were able to fully absorb the sight that stood before them: a goddess made entirely of light.

The goddess's name was Durga, and the gods decided to gift her with many powerful weapons. From Shiva she received a trident just like his own, while Vishwakarma, god of craftsmanship, offered an axe he had smelted himself. From Vishnu she obtained a discus and Varuna a razor-sharp spear. Vayu, god of the winds, created an impressive bow for the goddess, while Indra handed over one of his very own lightning bolts. Yama tore from his staff of death another just like it, and Brahma, god of creation, presented Durga with a set of the finest prayer beads to carry with her.

Finally, Kala, god of time, held up a sparkling sword and shield with which the goddess could defend herself in battle. However, she still required a steed, and so Himalaya, god of the mountains, presented her with a gigantic lion on which she could ride.

With a weapon in each hand, Durga looked around at the gathered gods and let forth a booming laugh. She was ready. Mounting her charge, the goddess sprang from the earth so forcefully that mountains shook beneath

her. Higher and higher she flew, until she could touch the heavens themselves. Meanwhile, the violent tremors Durga's journey sent through the universe alerted Mahishasura to the goddess's arrival.

The demon readied his followers for battle, confident he would once again prevail. Yet no matter how many arrows the asuras fired or swords they swung in the goddess' direction, she merely swept them aside with her hand. Wielding her own array of armaments, Durga pushed through the mass of Mahishasura's soldiers, leaving their bodies abandoned in her wake. When swords did manage to touch her skin, they simply shattered, unable to penetrate her dazzling form.

Finally, Mahishasura himself faced Durga in battle. The demon took on the guise of a gigantic buffalo and pawed the earth with his powerful hooves. Mahishasura laughed in the goddess's face, for how could she possibly defeat him?

His arrogance was his weakness, for he had forgotten the specifics of his immunity. With his horns, he raised the mountains from the earth and threw them at Durga with all his might. Yet, to his dismay, the goddess let forth a stream of arrows, destroying the projectiles in their path.

"You big-headed fool," Durga guffawed. "I am here to end your reign of terror. It is time to accept your fate."

With these words, Durga grabbed the buffalo by the horns and forced him to the ground. Holding him down by the neck she raised her sword and with all the strength that she possessed, severed Mahishasura's head from his neck. Finally, the demon was no more and the world was free. For while no man could defeat Mahishasura, this woman certainly could.

BE MORE LIKE DURGA

If you take away the giant lions and deadly swords, Durga's story is one where good champions over evil and one woman takes up a mantle that no one else has been able to before. The thing is, you don't have to be a warrior goddess to make a difference.

When it comes to the here and now, remember that you too have so much to contribute. You may even have something to bring to the table that no one else can. Whether you're passionate about the environment, education, healthcare or all of the above, do some research and find out what you can do to get involved.

Sometimes it might seem like there are plenty of people already involved in your passion, and you might even wonder what you could possibly offer. But never underestimate the importance of every individual when it comes to the fight for a better world. If everyone waited for someone else to do the work, then surely nothing would ever be achieved. So let's do it together.

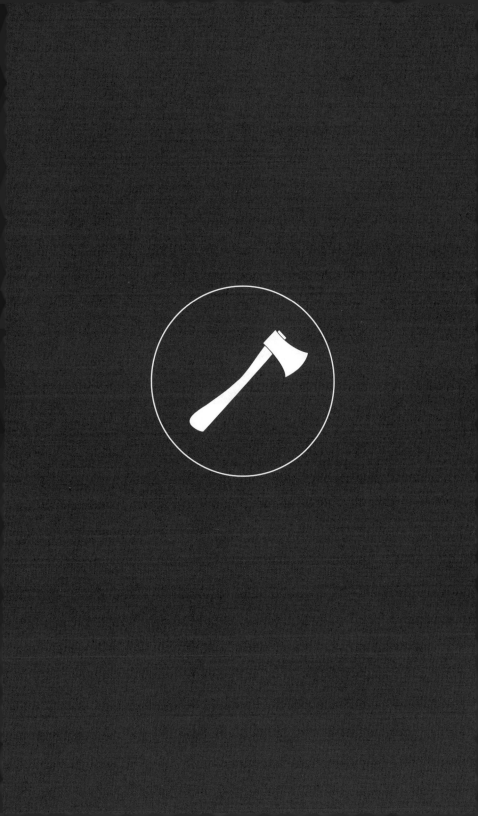

SHOOT FOR THE STARS LIKE HINA

NAME: HINA

ALSO KNOWN AS SINA INA-INARAM OR
HINA-MALAMALAMA

Has anyone ever told you your dreams are too big?

You shouldn't let them pull you down — and Hina's story might show you why.

WHO IS HINA?

Hina is a deity recognized across Polynesian cultures as ruling over many aspects of life, including the sea, but in Hawai'i, Tahiti and Samoa she is also known as the goddess of the moon. In Hawaiian, the word *mahina*, meaning moon, comes from the goddess's name. The Kalaupapa National Historical Park of Kalaupapa in Hawai'i is also home to the remains of the largest heiau (Hawaiian temple) dedicated to the goddess. In different Polynesian myths, Hina is often connected to the hero Māui, depicted as either his sister or his wife. Elsewhere the identity of her husband varies. In this tale she is married to a Hawaiian chief named Aikanaka.

HINA'S STORY

The goddess Hina lived alongside her husband, Aikanaka, chief of his people, at the base of the volcano Haleakalā. Hina was famous in her own right, however. She was known across all eight islands of Hawai'i for making the finest kapa, a popular fabric made from the toughest parts of trees and shrubs. Each day she rose early to soak the plant fibers she had gathered, before beating them with her i'e kuku (kapa beater) until they were thin and malleable. Hina's kapa was so soft and fine that everyone clamored to have their clothes made from her fabric over anyone else's.

It was hard work, and Hina toiled from dusk until dawn each day. Meanwhile, her husband, Aikanaka, grew lazier and more unpleasant as the years passed. This life, Hina realized, brought her no pleasure. She worked to the bone with a family who provided no support.

So Hina asked herself what it was she wanted. Surely there was more to life than this? And there it was—more! She wanted more, and why should she not have it? But then, what did more look like? Hina lay down on the earth, where she contemplated her future. As she pondered, she found herself gazing up at the darkening sky. She watched as the stars and planets twinkled and shone above her, beckoning her.

"Up there is my future," whispered Hina.

Hina decided that she would travel to the sun and trial its surface as her new home. After all, it was brighter than any other point in the sky and would surely be the most comfortable. From the clouds, she conjured a dazzling rainbow upon which she began her journey, each step taking her closer to her destination. But the further she walked, the stronger the sun's rays became.

Gradually, its blazing heat scorched her skin and weakened her resolve until it was unbearable. When finally she was unable to travel any further, the goddess conceded defeat, turning on her heel and sliding down the rainbow the way she had come. But now what? she

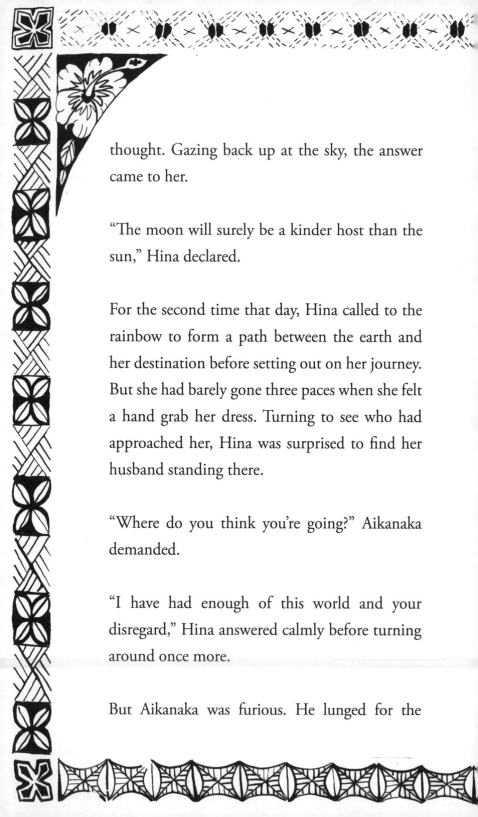

thought. Gazing back up at the sky, the answer came to her.

"The moon will surely be a kinder host than the sun," Hina declared.

For the second time that day, Hina called to the rainbow to form a path between the earth and her destination before setting out on her journey. But she had barely gone three paces when she felt a hand grab her dress. Turning to see who had approached her, Hina was surprised to find her husband standing there.

"Where do you think you're going?" Aikanaka demanded.

"I have had enough of this world and your disregard," Hina answered calmly before turning around once more.

But Aikanaka was furious. He lunged for the

goddess and grabbed hold of her ankle, holding on fast. Undeterred, Hina carried on walking, slowly but surely, trailing Aikanaka behind her. The higher she climbed, the more determined she grew, until she was shaking her leg so vigorously that Aikanaka's grip began to slip. In one last-ditch attempt to hold on, the chief squeezed so tightly Hina's leg broke in half. The calf and foot fell away, tumbling down the rainbow with Aikanaka in tow. Shocked but no less resolute, Hina continued on her journey, pulling a calabash (a large rounded fruit) from her bags to use as a crutch. As she walked, she sang the most powerful incantations she knew into the silence, and the sky itself watched over and encouraged her ascent.

Finally, after many hours, Hina arrived at her destination and found it to her liking. Here she would be happy, she told herself. And she was, watching over the people on earth from above and eventually finding a new husband who loved her as she deserved.

BE MORE LIKE HINA

It's safe to say I've taken a few liberties with the title of this chapter, naming it "shoot for the stars" when Hina actually travels to the moon. Yet, in a way, this perfectly encompasses the entire idea of this book.

When you read the stories of these incredible women, the expectation is not that you must emulate them literally or not at all. You may very well become an astronaut and stand on the moon, but there are more ways than one to shoot for the stars. Like Hina, you are entitled to dream and work towards those dreams whether others believe in them or not. Don't let anyone else set your expectations for you. Be the first in your family to go to university or write that story you can't forget. Audition for the role in that theatre show or take a business course and start your own company. That is how we can all be a little bit more like Hina. The journey won't always be easy, but I promise it's worth it.

PART TWO

LOOKING INWARD

LET IT OUT LIKE BRIGID

NAME: BRIGID

ALSO KNOWN AS ST. BRIGID, BRIGHID,
BRÌGHDE, BRIGIT OR BRÍG

Do you think that holding in your feelings makes you seem stronger?

Learn a lesson from Brigid's tale, which reminds us that our emotions are where our true strength lies.

WHO IS BRIGID?

Brigid is a member of the Tuatha Dé Danann, a fairy-like race of beings often worshipped as gods and goddesses in Celtic folk tradition. She was also later adopted by Christianity and became known as St. Brigid by Christian settlers in Ireland and Scotland. She was skilled in numerous crafts, including healing, midwifery and poetry. The annual pagan festival of Imbolc, which welcomes the arrival of spring on February 1st, is also used as an opportunity by many to celebrate the goddess Brigid. The same date is known as St. Brigid's Day in the Christian tradition.

BRIGID'S STORY

When the Tuatha Dé Danann came to Ireland, they found the land was occupied by a fearsome people known as the Fomorians. At first, the two races rubbed along as well as possible, although they generally kept to themselves. Then one day a young Tuatha Dé Danann woman called Ériu lay with Elatha, king of the Fomorians. Together they conceived a son and named him Bres. Because of the hostility between their two people, the two could not be together, and so Bres' mother was left to raise him on her own.

By the time Bres was fully grown he had become well-known among the Tuatha Dé Danann. He was both a skilled swordsman and more beautiful than any of his kin. His reputation was so great that when the Tuatha Dé Danann next decided to appoint a king, it was Bres they chose. Naturally, he was desired by many men and women, but it was Brigid, daughter of the Dagda, who loved him most. Fortunately for both, Bres returned her feelings and the two married.

Shortly into their marriage, Brigid gave birth to a son, and they named him Ruadán. While their lives seemed blissful at first, Brigid was unaware of how her people had grown to resent their king. Bres was a careless ruler, and the Tuatha Dé Danann's lives had grown hard and wearisome under his reign. Eventually, the Tuatha Dé Danann came to Bres and told him they would follow him no longer. Bres was furious, and no matter what Brigid said, his temper could not be tamed. Shrugging his wife aside, he set out for the kingdom of the Fomorians, taking with him their only son.

While Brigid still hoped for reconciliation, Bres was preparing for war. He rallied his father's troops, intent on bringing the Tuatha Dé Danann under Fomorian rule. Meanwhile, the Tuatha Dé Danann appointed a man named Lugh as king in Bres' place. War broke out between the two people and many men fell. But to the Fomorians' horror, while their soldiers died where they lay, the Tuatha Dé Danann's would rise again each morning as if reborn. Desperate to find out what trick the other side possessed, Bres decided to send Ruadán to investigate.

Donning a disguise, Ruadán snuck into the enemy camp to discover the Tuatha Dé Danann's secret. First, he spied the smithy Goibniu at work, shaping weapons of such strength and power that the wounds they inflicted could not be healed. Next, he followed the sound of chanting to find three men and one woman standing by a sacred well. Ruadán watched in awe as the healers threw the wounded body of a Tuatha Dé Danann man into its depths, chanting all the while. To the boy's shock, when the body was next pulled out, the man was healthy and whole once more. Running back to his father as fast as his legs would carry him, Ruadán told Bres of what he had seen.

"Good work, my son," Bres commended. "Now, take this spear and use it to kill one of them."

And so Ruadán made his way back to the Tuatha

Dé Danann camp, less careful than he had been before. When he arrived, he threw the spear, striking Goibniu in the side. The blow was not a deadly one, however, and the smith pulled the spear from his side only to hurl it back harder and faster at his attacker. The noise Ruadán made next echoed through the camp and found his mother's ears. Brigid recognized Ruadán's voice at once. She rushed to her son, but upon arrival was horrified to see the boy already lay dying in the dirt, his wound too deep to heal. Slumping down by his side, Brigid held her son's body in her arms. She then raised her head to the skies and let out the most pitiful wail. The depth of her pain was heard by Tuatha Dé Danann and Fomorians alike. Brigid howled and wept till her voice could take it no more, and she was left with only silent tears to shed. Never before had such a sound been heard throughout Ireland. Yet, from that day on, those who grieved were granted a way to express their sorrow, no longer forced to keep it inside. Some even say that it was Brigid's display of raw emotion which brought the fighting to an end.

BE MORE LIKE BRIGID

It can be tempting to bottle up those emotions that cause us the most pain and discomfort. I've experienced tough times when I've tried to push the hurt or sadness down, hoping the difficult feelings will just disappear—I'm sure you have too. But I know that this rarely leads to any positive resolution. Instead, the feelings only warp and transform, sometimes turning to rage or great sadness. Meanwhile, the original emotion becomes lost and much harder to address. While your first thought might be to tell the world you're fine as a demonstration of strength, know that being vulnerable is actually one of the strongest things you can do. Because only when we express our feelings can we learn from them or recover.

Whenever I need a reminder of this, I think of Brigid, who let her grief be heard across a battlefield. Life might hurt, it might be unfair, it might even be cruel, but you don't have to pretend none of this affects you. Let it out. Cry. Let the tears flow. Express whatever it is you're feeling. And if you need support, then talk to a friend or someone you trust, who can give you the space to explore and be heard.

THINK CREATIVELY
LIKE NÜWA

┌─ **NAME:** 女媧 (TRADITIONAL CHINESE) ─┐
└─ ALSO KNOWN AS NÜWA, NÜGUA OR EMPRESS HUANG ─┘

Struggling to find the solution to a seemingly impossible task? Why not come at it from a new angle like Nüwa did?

WHO IS NÜWA?

Nüwa is a serpent-bodied goddess in Chinese mythology who was partly responsible for the creation of the world. She and her brother Fuxi, whom she eventually married, lived together in the mythical Kunlun Shan mountain range. Nüwa was said to have molded the first humans out of clay. When this task became too time consuming, she instead began to trail long reels of string through the earth in order to mass produce the rest of humankind. Today, annual pilgrimages are still made to the Wā Huáng Palace in China's Hebei province in her honor.

NÜWA'S STORY

According to Chinese mythology, when the world was first created, four gigantic pillars were erected to hold the sky above the earth and ensure balance between the two realms. The gods and goddesses themselves were not always peaceful and would often fight. Finally, a day came when their fighting caused the pillars to suffer seemingly irreparable damage.

Without the support of the four pillars, heaven slipped from its position, and the earth was left exposed. Uncovered, the nine provinces of China fell into chaos. Fires burned across the landscape and could not be extinguished. Animals and birds began acting strange and snatched humans from the streets. And the black dragon who controlled the seas allowed his waters to spill into towns and flood the humans' homes.

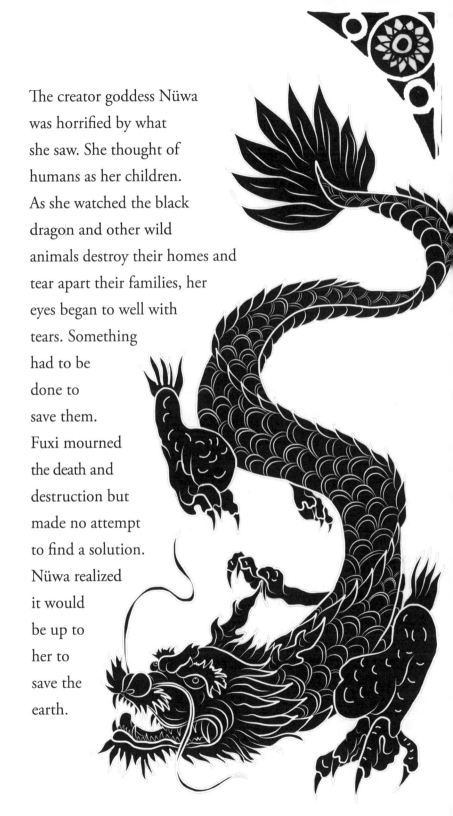

The creator goddess Nüwa was horrified by what she saw. She thought of humans as her children. As she watched the black dragon and other wild animals destroy their homes and tear apart their families, her eyes began to well with tears. Something had to be done to save them. Fuxi mourned the death and destruction but made no attempt to find a solution. Nüwa realized it would be up to her to save the earth.

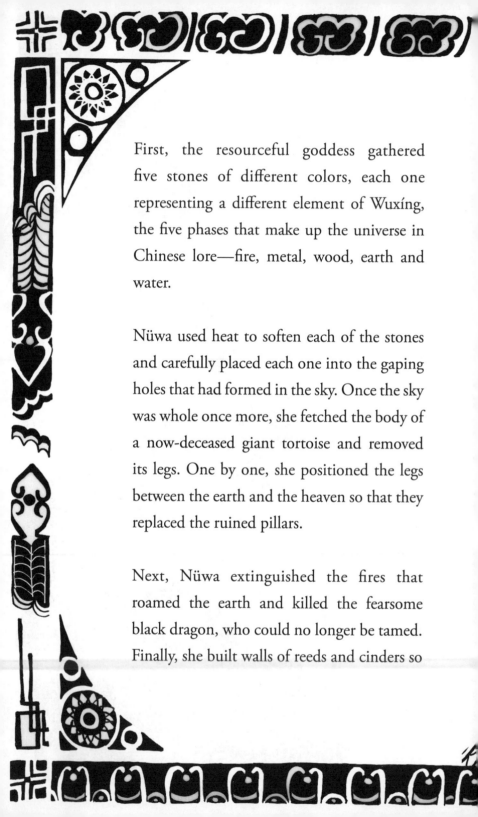

First, the resourceful goddess gathered five stones of different colors, each one representing a different element of Wuxíng, the five phases that make up the universe in Chinese lore—fire, metal, wood, earth and water.

Nüwa used heat to soften each of the stones and carefully placed each one into the gaping holes that had formed in the sky. Once the sky was whole once more, she fetched the body of a now-deceased giant tortoise and removed its legs. One by one, she positioned the legs between the earth and the heaven so that they replaced the ruined pillars.

Next, Nüwa extinguished the fires that roamed the earth and killed the fearsome black dragon, who could no longer be tamed. Finally, she built walls of reeds and cinders so that the water was forced to return to the sea. With order restored, the humans watched as the once-rabid animals fled their villages, and together they rejoiced. The goddess had saved them all. So, thanks to clever Nüwa, balance was returned to the nine provinces of China, and the humans lived in peace one more.

BE MORE LIKE NÜWA

When a problem seems overwhelming, I often think about Nüwa. While Nüwa may not be here to solve our problems, we can still take a leaf out of her book and think outside the box. Take a step back and look at the things from a different angle, literally or metaphorically. It might be something you've been working on yourself or an issue someone else has asked for help in solving. Either way, just remember the goddess's story.

When faced with a problem the other gods thought insurmountable, Nüwa was able to offer a new approach. She recycled objects around her and reused them in new ways. Sometimes it's the simplest solution that eludes us when we're stressed or panicking. Other times the idea you come up with might be unconventional or surprising. But like Nüwa, you'll never know until you give it a try.

STAND YOUR GROUND LIKE DEMETER

NAMES: Δημήτηρ (GREEK ALPHABET)
— ALSO KNOWN AS DEMETER OR DEO —

Struggling to find the courage to fight for what you want? Learn from Demeter how to stand your ground.

WHO IS DEMETER?

Demeter is the ancient Greek goddess of agriculture and the harvest. She was one of the twelve Olympians in Greek religion—important gods and goddesses who were believed to reside on Mount Olympus.

Many children are attributed to her but none so consistently or famously as Persephone, goddess of spring and Demeter's daughter by the god Zeus. Both mother and daughter were celebrated in ancient Greece during an annual three-day festival in Athens known as the Thesmophoria, attended exclusively by women.

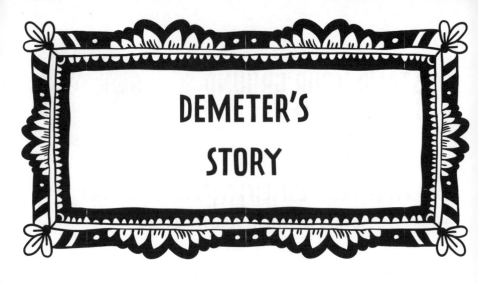

DEMETER'S STORY

One fateful afternoon, Persephone was picking wildflowers with the Oceanid nymphs, daughters of Oceanus, when she spotted a singular narcissus flower that had sprung from the soil. As the goddess bent to pluck the exquisite bloom, the earth beneath her began to rupture. A gigantic crack opened in the ground and from it rose Hades, atop his horse-drawn carriage. Before Persephone could react, the god grabbed her around her waist and dragged her down into his kingdom.

The goddess's screams rang throughout the meadows, calling out for either of her parents to save her. Demeter, who was out of sight but not of earshot, heard her daughter's cries and immediately came running. But by the time she arrived, it was too late. Both the crack in the ground and her daughter had disappeared, leaving no sign of where she had gone. Demeter stormed Olympus looking for answers, but none of the gods or goddesses she asked would reveal her daughter's fate; they were more afraid of offending Hades than upsetting Demeter.

Desperate, Demeter ceased to wash or eat and instead roamed the land calling out for someone to help. Finally, after ten days had passed, the goddess Hekate came to her.

"Dear Demeter, I did not see who took your daughter, but I think I know who might have. Helios, as the sun, sees all that happens beneath him. Let us visit him together and ask him what he knows."

So the two women approached the Titan god of the sun and, to Demeter's luck, Helios proved most forthcoming.

"It was Hades who stole your daughter, but do not fret—he is a good match for Persephone. He is well revered and Zeus approves of the match."

"What do I care about Zeus's feelings on the matter?" Demeter retorted. "He can marry Hades himself if he thinks so highly of him. My daughter did not consent to this union; you heard her screams yourself. Hades has taken Persephone against her will and trapped her in his kingdom. Yet you suggest I might be pleased for them. Enough!"

Demeter was not about to back down, and if Zeus would not willingly help her, she would show him what she was willing to do. Abandoning the other deities, Demeter refused to return to Olympus. Instead, she spent her days roaming the earth and bringing destruction down upon it. For it was Demeter who brought the land to life. Without her, the soil grew arid and infertile. Nothing would grow and famine ravaged the land. Over the course of a dreadful year, humans starved and animals perished without Demeter's blessing. Eventually, Zeus himself pleaded with the goddess to rethink her path. But Demeter stood her ground. The king of the gods offered her many gifts, and each one was refused. Not until she saw her daughter would anything else

on earth grow again. Finally, Zeus recognized defeat.

"If Persephone has refrained from eating anything the underworld has to offer, then she may return to you," Zeus declared, sending Hermes to inform the lord of the dead.

Meanwhile, in Hades' realm, Persephone was racked with sorrow. All that she loved had been taken from her, and her imprisonment beneath the surface of the earth had made her heart so heavy that she had not sampled a single bite of food. Then, one evening, the god of the underworld came to her room with a grave look upon his face.

"Do not cry any longer, Persephone; you shall be allowed to leave this place. Go back to your mother and the world above, but I ask you to consider returning to me while you are there."

Hades smiled softly and offered the girl something from his hand. "Before you go, however, please eat something, for I hate to see you look so wan."

He handed her a pomegranate. Overjoyed at Hades' news, Persephone jumped upon the fruit and ate to her heart's content. Hades, however, had told a lie. He knew that by eating the fruit, Persephone would be bound to the underworld forever. And so the devious god brought Persephone back to the world of the living to meet with her mother and father, failing to inform her of what he'd done.

"My daughter," Demeter cried upon seeing Hades' carriage arrive.

"Don't celebrate too soon," Hades called to her, turning to look at Zeus. "The goddess here beside me has consumed fruit of the underworld, therefore she rightfully belongs with me."

"Is this true?" asked Zeus.

"It is, father," Persephone wailed, realizing how Hades had tricked her.

"Zeus, if my daughter is forced to return to the underworld, I will abandon your people once more," Demeter bellowed. "Who will make sacrifices to you or rub your ego should humanity all die?" Zeus considered this idea.

"Here is my compromise for everyone involved," he began. "Persephone will live on earth with her mother for three quarters of the year. During winter, when the days are short and darkness prevails, she will return to Hades as his wife and rule the underworld by his side."

Looking towards their daughter, both Demeter and Zeus watched as Persephone nodded her head. At least this way, Persephone thought, she would be able to spend the warmer months in the company of her mother and friends. So Demeter also agreed, taking her lead from the daughter she had fought so hard to defend. From then on, the goddess Persephone would live on earth during spring and summer, and part of autumn, returning to the underworld for the rest of autumn and all of winter to rule as its queen. And Demeter had made this possible by standing her ground.

BE MORE LIKE DEMETER

Next time something means a lot to you, remember to channel your inner Demeter and don't back down! It might feel difficult, especially when it feels as though everyone else is against you, but if you believe strongly enough in what you're fighting for, it is important to stand your ground. You might be asking for respect or to be taken more seriously, or you might be defending someone or something you think has been wronged.

Whatever the situation, don't let anyone dismiss you because it's easier than listening to what you have to say. I'm not saying you have to unleash a year-long famine upon the earth for others to hear you, but simply trust your own convictions and speak them loud and clear. In the end, you might have to compromise a little like Demeter did, or you may be surprised to find that your confidence is so convincing that you achieve exactly what you wanted. Either way, the result can only be better than doing nothing at all.

CARRY ON LIKE THE SUN

NAME: ᎤᎤᏔᏏᎡᎯ (CHEROKEE)
ALSO KNOWN AS THE SUN

Struggling to find the motivation to face the day?

Let the Sun's story remind you how important it is to keep going.

WHO IS THE SUN?

Many Indigenous tribes in America identify the sun as a man, such as the Hopi sun spirit Tawa and the Navajo sun god Tsohanoai. This is not the case for the Cherokee Nation, however, who in their various mythologies identify the sun as a female deity. The Cherokee people make up one of the two largest Indigenous tribes in present-day USA, alongside the Navajo, and are primarily located in north-eastern Oklahoma. In the following story, the sun is imagined as an older woman with a fully grown daughter of her own.

THE SUN'S STORY

Each day the Sun would traverse the sky, mapping an enormous arc across the earth, before finally turning in for the night. At the point where her path reached its peak was her daughter's home. So, naturally, when the Sun reached the midpoint of her journey each day, she would stop and pay a visit to her child. They would sit and talk, always pleased with each other's company.

There was one thing that consumed the Sun's mind. She hated how the humans looked at her, always scowling and scrunching up their eyes. In contrast, when they gazed upon her brother, the Moon, their expressions were happy and serene. Eventually, the Sun grew so angry with humankind that she decided a punishment was in order. The next day, when she arrived at her daughter's house, she settled by the door, ready for a longer visit.

There the Sun remained for weeks, only retreating inside her daughter's home briefly each day. She shone down on the earth, never giving the people below an ounce of respite from her heat. The plants began to wither, and bodies of water dried up. The humans grew tired and hungry, and their skin burned under the Sun's constant glare.

The humans grew desperate for they were dying in the hundreds, and so they sought the help of the Yunwi Tsunsdi, good spirits who knew the art of magic. Happy to help, the Yunwi Tsunsdi created a concoction that turned two of the men into snakes, one the spreading adder and the other a copperhead. The snakes were then sent to lie in wait for the Sun by her daughter's door. But when the Sun revealed herself, the two snakes were blinded by her brightness. The copperhead spat venom, but it was ineffective, while the spreading adder slithered away. With their first attempt proving unsuccessful, they realized they would have to try again.

This time, the Yunwi Tsunsdi turned one of the men into a rattlesnake and sent him on his quest. The rattlesnake bided his time, waiting for the door to open. As soon as it did, he struck without looking. But when he opened his eyes, he was horrified to see not the Sun but her daughter lying dead upon the ground. The rattlesnake fled, but the Sun had heard the disturbance and quickly came to see what had happened. When she found her daughter's body, still and empty of life, she let out a heart-wrenching moan that reverberated through the skies.

Overwhelmed by her grief, the Sun retreated to her daughter's home and closed the door behind her. Here she passed her days mourning the child she had lost. The earth ceased to burn, but without the Sun, it grew dark and melancholy. The humans were racked with guilt over their role in the Sun's misery, so once again they approached the Yunwi Tsunsdi to ask for help.

"If you wish the Sun to rise once more, you must retrieve her daughter from the land of the dead." The spirits then handed over a small wooden box. "With this you will be able to capture the young woman's spirit and bring her home. But remember, you must not open the box again until you have returned. Not even a peek."

The humans gratefully accepted the spirit's gift and set out to the land of the dead that same day. They traveled for seven days and seven nights, although there was never any break in the oppressive darkness around them. Finally, they arrived at their destination and found the spirits of the dead dancing as happily as the living did back home. They swung around in great circles, laughing and singing with each other all the while, and at first, the humans could not tell one from another. However, as they watched, their features became clearer, until one man spotted the Sun's daughter smiling on the edge of the outermost circle.

Using the spirit's vessel as they had been instructed, the humans trapped the Sun's daughter inside and began their journey back to the land of the living. But a few days into their travels, they heard a voice call out from the box they carried.

"Please, let me out," the Sun's daughter cried. "I am terribly hungry."

Heeding the spirit's warning, the humans ignored her shouts and carried on. Yet she did not let up. Next, she called that she was thirsty, but they ignored that too. Finally, when they were less than a day from the her house, the girl pleaded that they open the box just a crack, for she was struggling to breathe. This was the final straw. Terrified they might kill the Sun's daughter a second time, the humans lifted the container lid just enough that fresh air might enter. Even the tiniest opening was enough to break the spell, and out flew a tiny red bird that quickly vanished into the distance. The box was left empty.

Devasted by their error, the humans knew they owed the Sun the truth. They arrived at the door to her daughter's house and told her their sorry tale. Upon learning of how close her daughter had been, the Sun began to weep anew. Her tears fell fast and heavy, threatening to flood the earth below. This was it; she knew her daughter was really gone. All this time there had been a tiny part of her unwilling to accept what happened, but no longer.

The humans offered the Sun whatever comfort she needed and as time passed, they sent their most skilled performers to dance and sing before her, recounting tales to make her smile and telling jokes that made her laugh. Although the pain did not vanish immediately, as she sat and listened to the humans' stories, the Sun was reminded there was still yet more joy to be found.

BE MORE LIKE THE SUN

When the Sun's losses felt impossible to bear, her first instinct was to cut herself off from the rest of the world—an instinct I'm all too familiar with. When I lost my dad, I felt adrift and confused; how was I supposed to keep going? But what I learned is that sometimes, just waking up to meet each new day is the bravest thing we can do—like the sun rising each morning in the sky. Things might seem hard or even impossible, but tomorrow may look different, you just have to wait to see.

Whether something big has happened in your life that leads to sorrow or you're going through something internally that you can't put your finger on, it's important to give yourself time. Time to feel, time to grieve and time to heal. So cut yourself some slack, celebrate the small victories and relish the little joys of life, even if they're short lived. Step outside your head or your bedroom and let others be there for you, like the humans were there for the Sun in the end.

There will be times ahead when it will be easier, but in the meantime there is no reason you have to be alone. Like the Sun, you will eventually find the smile that's waiting deep inside.

PERSEVERE LIKE ISIS

NAMES: 𓊨𓏏𓁦 (EGYPTIAN HIEROGLYPHICS)
ALSO KNOWN AS ISIS OR ESET

Do you feel as though a new hurdle seems to crop up at every turn? Isis's story of determination might help you find the energy to keep jumping them.

WHO IS ISIS?

Isis is the ancient Egyptian goddess of healing and magic. She had a son named Horus with her husband and a brother named Osiris, god of the dead, whom she loved dearly. Throughout Egyptian mythology, she can be seen fiercely protecting both her husband and son. This loyalty even extended to her nephew and adopted son, Anubis, whom she rescued and raised as her own after her sister Nephthys abandoned him. She was one of the most popular and powerful deities in ancient Egyptian religion, and over time she was also introduced to ancient Greek religion thanks to Egyptian immigration.

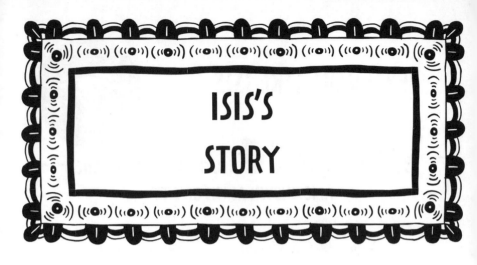

ISIS'S STORY

Isis and Osiris had ruled the world successfully for many years—showing humanity how to build cities and grow their own food. Although the people loved them, their brother Set could not help but resent them, and he grew jealous of Osiris's power. Why should he not have his turn at being king?

Unfortunately for Set, Osiris was not about to abdicate his throne, nor were the people inclined to rebel against their ruler. Set knew that he would have to seize his power by force. But first, he must separate Osiris from his queen, for Isis was a formidable foe.

So Set had a casket made of stone and adorned with gold and gems until it dazzled. The container was to be the centerpiece at an extravagant party, to which only Set's closest friends and Osiris were invited. When the celebrations were in full swing, Set announced a contest: whomever fit inside the casket the best could keep it for themselves. One by one the party guests took their turn at laying inside the casket, but none of them fit quite right. Eventually came Osiris' turn and with his arms tucked to his sides and his legs stretched out straight, he discovered the box was exactly his size. But before the god had a chance to rejoice, the lid was slammed down and molten lead was poured over the vessel to seal it shut. With his brother now trapped inside, Set had his followers take the casket and throw it carelessly into the river Nile.

After a few days had passed and Osiris had not returned home, Isis grew concerned. She began to roam their palace in search of information concerning his whereabouts.

Finally, she came upon two small children who informed her of a jeweled casket they had seen trapped in the roots of a tree by the river Nile. Immediately suspicious, Isis followed their directions and found the box. Certain of what the casket must contain, she heaved it free with all her strength and returned it to her chambers, where she planned to find a way to set Osiris free.

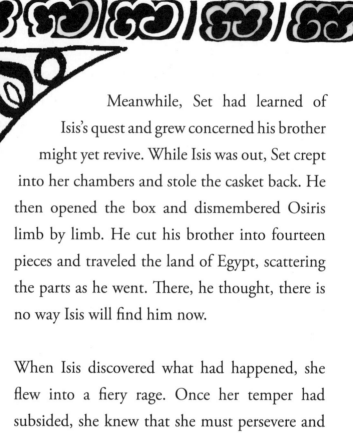

Meanwhile, Set had learned of Isis's quest and grew concerned his brother might yet revive. While Isis was out, Set crept into her chambers and stole the casket back. He then opened the box and dismembered Osiris limb by limb. He cut his brother into fourteen pieces and traveled the land of Egypt, scattering the parts as he went. There, he thought, there is no way Isis will find him now.

When Isis discovered what had happened, she flew into a fiery rage. Once her temper had subsided, she knew that she must persevere and retrieve Osiris's body once more. Gathering her wits about her, she set sail across the rivers and swamps of Egypt, gathering the pieces of her husband. Eventually, there was but one part she could not find: Osiris' phallus. This was because it had been consumed by the fish who swam beneath the water. Isis, however, was not to be deterred. Using her magical gifts, she crafted a replacement piece and reassembled

Osiris's body upon a giant stone table.

Isis then approached her nephew Anubis, whose job it was to care for the bodies of the dead. As Isis watched, Anubis began to wrap the body parts in one long, continuous piece of white linen, binding them tightly together once more. While he worked, Isis chanted every spell of healing that she knew.

When the last bandage had been wrapped around Osiris's head and the goddess had murmured her final spell, the magic was complete. Both Isis and Anubis watched the mummy with bated breath until suddenly, the fully bandaged figure of Osiris raised his head from the table. Isis ran to her husband's side and wrapped her arms around his newly restored body.

"You have returned to me!" She cried.

"Not for long, I'm afraid to say," Osiris replied, a sad smile on his face.

"What do you mean?" Isis demanded.

"While I was gone, I visited the underworld and witnessed chaos among our people there. The dead need a ruler just as the living do, my love. You have done me a great honor in undoing Set's evil, but now you must give my body a proper farewell so I can return to the land of the dead once more." Tears slid down Isis' cheeks. She would miss Osiris with her entire being, but she also knew that what he was doing was right and just.

"Before you go, allow us one last night together so that we might conceive an heir."

And so ten months later Isis gave birth to a boy. The child's name was Horus and over the years Isis protected him fiercely from Set until he was ready to take his father's throne.

BE MORE LIKE ISIS

What is it they say? If at first you don't succeed, try, try again. Well, I don't know who "they" are, but this certainly appears to be Isis's mantra. As nice as it would be, first attempts don't always succeed, but that doesn't mean it's time to give up. Sometimes perseverance is key.

Whether you are trying to figure out your future or picking up knitting as a new hobby, don't be deterred if your first choice of internship turns you down or your woollen scarf starts to inexplicably unravel halfway through. Submit another application, find a new approach or pick those knitting needles back up and start at the beginning again.

After all, if Isis had given up at the first, second or even third hurdle in her quest, she would never have had another night with her husband or conceived her beloved son.

DEMAND RESPECT LIKE OṢUN

NAME: OṢUN
ALSO KNOWN AS OSHÚN OR OXAM

Have the prejudices of others made you doubt yourself? If so, Oṣun's solidarity might be exactly what you need right now.

WHO IS OṢUN?

Oṣun is an orisha, a divine spirit which forms part of numerous religious practices by the African diaspora and which occupies a space between the creator god Olorun and humanity. Oṣun is particularly important to the Ifá religion of the Yoruba people, which is practiced across Africa and the Caribbean. She is primarily perceived as a manifestation of the divine feminine (the idea that we all have a goddess inside of us), and she is associated with beauty, love and fertility. According to some traditions, she is also a spirit of the river, a space full of potential. For many modern-day practitioners she is a symbol of female empowerment and liberation.

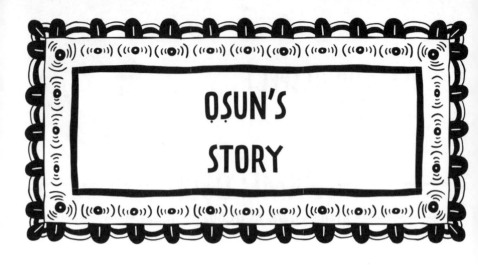

OṢUN'S STORY

Olorun, the supreme creator, had spent a long time making the world to his own design, yet as he looked upon the final product, he knew there was still more work to be done. The humans who lived on earth were careless and irresponsible. They wasted what they had and took little care of the world around them. It was clear to Olorun that if humankind were to survive, they must learn to live better lives. So the god gathered his orisha, the divinities who assisted him at every turn, and sent them down to earth. Among their number was one woman, the goddess Oṣun.

When they arrived on earth, the orisha gathered to discuss their plans for earth's improvements. Each day, they came together to combine their knowledge, but one orisha was barred from their meetings: Oṣun.

As the only woman of their number, she was excluded from their discussions. Despite this, she returned each day, only for the other orisha to turn her away. Some asked, what could she possibly know that they did not know already? She will upset the balance of the world with her feminine energy, whispered others. Regardless of their reasoning, they were united in their prejudice.

Ọṣun grew angrier with each dismissal of her presence. Finally, fed up with the other orisha, she sought out the company of the wise women known as Àjé to the Yoruba people, who are similar to witches.

"You were right to come to us, sister, for we know your pain," the Àjé told her. "The men pay little heed to what we have to offer, and they dismiss our experiences as irrelevant to them."

"They will come to regret their ignorance, I suspect," Ọṣun replied.

Meanwhile, the other orisha found themselves at a loss. No matter what they did, order eluded them, and the world only fell deeper into chaos. Disease and drought swept the land and children ceased to be born. Food was scarce and humans fought among themselves day and night. Finally, they approached Ọlọrun and begged him to help.

"But where is Ọṣun?" the god asked.

"We sent her away," one of the orisha answered. "She is only a woman, after all; she would have gotten in our way."

"Is that so?" Ọlọrun scoffed. "Well, you better invite her to return if you hope to get anything done."

Humiliated, the orisha returned to earth and sought out the goddess they had dismissed.

"Please, Ọṣun, won't you forgive us? We need your help after all," they pleaded.

"Why should I join your number when you have shown me no respect? You scorned me for my sex and now you expect me to return simply because it suits you at last." Ọṣun scowled at the other orisha.

"We have seen the error in our ways, we swear it!" they responded desperately. "What can we do to prove it?"

"If you have truly left your misogyny behind you, then these are my demands. In the new order we create together, women will be equal to men. No woman shall be excluded from any meetings or sacred ceremonies. Women shall play a part in deciding the fate of humankind, just as men do now. And this must apply to all my sisters, not just me alone." With these words, she gave a nod in the direction of the Àjé, and the witches smiled in return.

Without hesitation, the other orisha agreed, and finally, by working together on equal ground, they were able to bring peace to humankind.

BE MORE LIKE ỌṢUN

It frustrates me to say that the experience of Ọṣun is one I'm familiar with. There have been multiple occasions in my life when my opinions or expertise have been diminished or dismissed simply because I am a woman. But no matter what, we are all as worthy of respect as anyone else. This is one of the reasons why I have so much admiration for Ọṣun.

In the face of prejudice, Ọṣun never doubts this indisputable fact. She finds solidarity with others who have been excluded and belittled, and when the time comes, she stands up for them all. When the other gods came to beg Ọṣun for her help, the goddess could easily have forgotten their sexism and accepted the power they offered her. But Ọṣun knew that nothing would ever truly change if she did not demand respect for herself and all women from that day on. So, while it might not always be easy, I try my hardest to do the same in my own life, and I hope that you will too. Sometimes discrimination is loud and other times it is subtle, but whatever the case, don't shy away from demanding the respect you deserve.

PRACTICE PATIENCE LIKE TĀRĀ

NAMES: तारा (SANSKRIT)
ALSO KNOWN AS TĀRĀ, SGROL-MA OR YESHE DAWA

Frustrated at having to wait to achieve your goals? Tārā's tale might help you appreciate that wait.

WHO IS TĀRĀ?

According to various Buddhist traditions, Tārā is either a bodhisattva, someone on the path to Buddhahood, or a fully enlightened Buddha. To become enlightened means to move beyond the cycle of rebirth that all living things are a part of according to Buddhist teachings.

In Buddhism, almost anyone can attain Buddhahood through dedication, although the most famous Buddha is probably the religion's founder, Siddhartha Gautam. Tārā is particularly respected as an expert in meditation, and many Buddhist practitioners look to her for guidance in their own self-reflection.

TĀRĀ'S STORY

Before she was Tārā, the bodhisattva was known as Yeshe Dawa. She had always been an intelligent and compassionate woman, and thus it seemed only natural that she decided to dedicate herself to the search for enlightenment. For through enlightenment, she knew, she could better the lives of all living beings. And so she came to learn from the Buddha Tathāgata with a selfless and open mind.

For more than ten million years, Yeshe Dawa followed Tathāgata's teachings, made countless offers to the Buddha and spent hours in meditation. Her dedication was so absolute that she eventually reached a level of concentration she had never before achieved; her mind had awoken, and she had taken the first step to enlightenment. It was then that she was approached by a group of men who were also followers of the Buddha.

"Your commitment has brought you far, Yeshe Dawa," one man said. "We did not expect a woman to come this far."

"Pray that next you might be reborn as a man like us," said another. "For surely only then you will be able to reach the ultimate state of enlightenment."

"What has my sex got to do with it?" replied Yeshe Dawa. "Male or female are meaningless terms in Buddhism. While some may waste their energy wishing to be reborn as men, my only wish is to lead us all from the cycle of rebirth altogether."

Ignoring the men and their uninvited advice, Yeshe Dawa continued to practice her faith as she had before, devoting herself to the teachings of the Buddha. As each year passed, her mind awakened further until over another ten million years had passed. She learned perseverance and kindness, wisdom and patience, and finally concentration. It was only then that Yeshe Dawa achieved enlightenment—through her own merit and dedication. Upon hearing this news, the Buddha Tathāgata praised her patience and commitment, declaring to the world that from that day on, Yesha Dawa would be known as the goddess Tārā to all.

BE MORE LIKE TĀRĀ

I would be lying if I claimed to be the world's most patient person. When I want something, I often want it now and the wait can feel unbearable. Sometimes a little bit of impatience might even be the thing that gets you going. It is important to remember, though, that sometimes patience is exactly what you need to practice. It can't be tomorrow today, after all.

Just as Tārā did not expect to achieve enlightenment after one year of meditation, you shouldn't expect to play the piano like Debussy after one month of lessons or land a triple axel after two weeks of ice skating. Expecting immediate success might even be detrimental to your efforts if you let its absence get you down. On the other hand, patience and dedication will get you where you want to be. You might even enjoy the journey that little bit more if you're not so caught up in the destination.

PART THREE

LOOKING TO OTHERS

LEND A HELPING HAND LIKE THE SIMORGH

NAME: سیمرغ (FARSI)

ALSO KNOWN AS SIMORGH, SIMURGH OR SĪMURĞ

Wondering how to help your friends or your wider community?

The Simorgh reminds us that there are simple ways in which we can all make a difference.

WHO IS THE SIMORGH?

The Simorgh is a giant legendary bird from Persian mythology. Although primarily described as a bird in the Persian texts, she is occasionally depicted with the head of a dog and the claws of lion. According to the Persian epic, the *Shahnameh*, the Simorgh was created by the Islamic God himself. She has lived on earth for many thousands of years and witnessed the passage of countless civilizations. Over millennia, the Simorgh is believed to have gained a great wealth of knowledge and wisdom, some of which she shares with the legendary hero Zāl in Persian mythology.

THE SIMORGH'S STORY

According to legend, there once lived a Persian hero named Sām, who ruled the ancient kingdom of Zavolistan, now part of modern-day Afghanistan. Sām had a son named Zāl who was born with albinism. When his son's fair hair and skin were revealed to him, Sām's actions were guided by prejudice. He had the baby taken from his kingdom and left exposed in the mountains where the great Simorgh made her nest.

Later that day, the Simorgh set out to fetch food for her children, who were not yet old enough to fly themselves. As she scoured the mountainside, she was surprised to see something small and wriggling out of the corner of her eye. Circling closer, she recognized the creature for what it was: a human baby. The Simorgh wondered, who would so cruelly leave an infant exposed to the harsh midday sun? Not she. The great bird nodded.

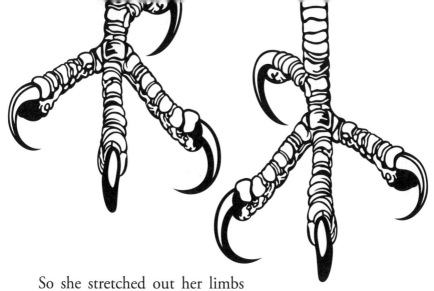

So she stretched out her limbs
and scooped the child up in
her giant claws.

From that day, the Simorgh raised Zāl as her own, feeding
and caring for him as she did her own chicks. Over the
years, Zāl grew tall and strong, until he was a no longer
a child but a fine young man who clambered across his
rocky home with dexterity and ease. Meanwhile, his
unusual presence did not go unnoticed by the travelers
who passed through the mountains each month. The
sight was so astonishing that they told tales of the man
they witnessed living in the mountains, watched over
by the divine Simorgh. Eventually, these stories reached
the ears of the king. Sām knew instinctively that this
mysterious young man was in fact the son that he had
so carelessly abandoned, and he was confronted by

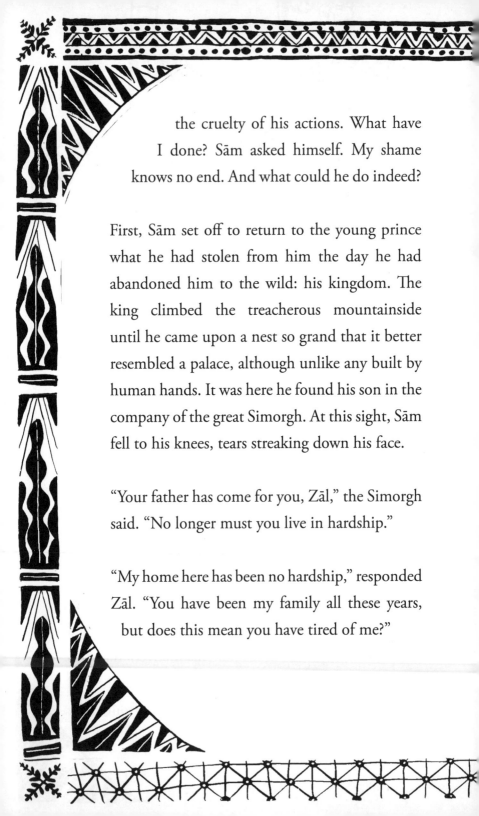

the cruelty of his actions. What have I done? Sām asked himself. My shame knows no end. And what could he do indeed?

First, Sām set off to return to the young prince what he had stolen from him the day he had abandoned him to the wild: his kingdom. The king climbed the treacherous mountainside until he came upon a nest so grand that it better resembled a palace, although unlike any built by human hands. It was here he found his son in the company of the great Simorgh. At this sight, Sām fell to his knees, tears streaking down his face.

"Your father has come for you, Zāl," the Simorgh said. "No longer must you live in hardship."

"My home here has been no hardship," responded Zāl. "You have been my family all these years, but does this mean you have tired of me?"

"I have done no such thing, dear boy, but these mortal riches belong to you. Whether you forgive your father is for you to decide. Do not think I would abandon you, however." The bird bent her neck and plucked three feathers from her plumage. "Take these with you and know you are always under my protection. If you should ever need me, all you need do is throw one of these feathers into a fire and I will come to bring you home."

And so Zāl returned to the kingdom of Zavolistan, where he reconciled with his father. As time passed, Zāl grew to be a wise and learned ruler, eventually taking over the role of king from his father. He took as his queen the princess Rudabeh, whom he loved dearly and she him in return.

Not long into their marriage, however, Rudabeh fell pregnant. Her pregnancy was not an easy one. Every day Rudabeh grew more ill, unable to sleep or eat as the child's birth grew closer. Finally, a day came when the queen fainted, and the palace went into a state of frenzy. What was to be done?

Zāl, however, had not forgotten the gift the great Simorgh had given him. He had a fire lit and into it he threw the first of his three feathers. At once the mighty bird appeared before him.

"Do not weep, child," the Simorgh said. "Your wife will live and birth a happy child yet. Simply do as I instruct. Fetch a priest skilled in healing and have him bring a cleaned and sharpened knife. Give Rudabeh your finest wine to dull the pain, for next your priest must open her belly. With care, the baby should be removed before your wife's wound is cleaned and sewn shut again. You must then apply a poultice of herbs, which I will instruct you how to make. Finally, take this feather of mine and place it on her side."

And, just as before,
the Simorgh plucked one of
her own feathers from her back and gifted
it to her adopted son.

Zāl and his healers followed the Simorgh's instructions to the letter, and with their help, Rudabeh birthed a brilliant baby boy. The queen still required much rest from her ordeal, but the great bird had spoken the truth and Rudabeh was well once more. The new parents named their son Rostam and festivities were held throughout the kingdom to celebrate his arrival. All thanks to the kindness and care of the magnificent Simorgh.

BE MORE LIKE THE SIMORGH

Sometimes we need to slow down and look beyond ourselves to see when others are struggling or in need of help. If you pause and take in your surroundings, you're likely to find someone who might need your help, whether they're a friend or someone else. You don't have to be a mythical bird to offer up a helping hand. Nor do you have to adopt an abandoned baby from a cliffside to make a difference. You could donate food and clothes that you don't need, or commit your time to a worthy cause. Helping others could be as simple as listening to a friend's problems and offering some practical advice or comforting them with a cup of tea. Any action, no matter how small, might make the world of difference to someone else. As long as you are respectful and considerate of what that person needs, just showing up like the Simorgh can be the most helpful thing you could ever do.

SET BOUNDARIES LIKE FREYJA

Do you find it hard to just say no? Learn from an expert like Freyja, who unapologetically puts her foot down!

WHO IS FREYJA?

Freyja is the Norse goddess of love and war, among other things. She is also a member of the Vanir tribe, one of two tribes of Norse deities alongside the Æsir. Freyja rules over the afterlife fields known as Fólkvangr. There she receives half of the souls of those who die in battle, while the other half join Odin in Valhalla. She is also skilled in the magical art of seiðr, which can be used to see into and influence the future.

FREYJA'S STORY

One morning in Asgard, the kingdom of the Norse gods, Thor, god of thunder, awoke to discover his precious hammer, Mjölnir, had disappeared. When wielded by the god, Mjölnir possessed great power, ensuring that Thor's aim would always be true and he would never miss his target. Thor was at a loss without it, but no matter how hard he looked, he could not find his beloved weapon. In despair, Thor let out a baleful moan that reverberated through the palace halls. His cries reached the ears of the crafty trickster god Loki, who came to see what was amiss.

"Mjölnir is gone," Thor howled. "Some crook has stolen my hammer while I slept."

"Well then, to Freyja we go!" Loki grinned, for he loved a mystery.

When the two men arrived at the goddess Freyja's chambers, they explained Thor's predicament to her. Then, Loki proposed a solution.

"Allow me to borrow your feathered cloak, Freyja, and I will find the missing hammer!"

"If my cloak can help, then consider it yours, for I know how important Mjölnir is to Thor," Freyja agreed, handing over the luxurious garment.

With the cloak around his shoulders, Loki was able to take to the skies. He flew above each of the nine realms in search of Mjölnir. Even with his bird's eye view it seemed at first as though his quest was doomed. That was until he soared over the kingdom of the giants and spied Thrym, their king, sat atop a mound of earth.

"Hail, Thrym, ogre king; I come in search of Mjölnir, Thor's beloved hammer," Loki announced, landing at the foot of the mound.

"Then you have come to the right place, trickster,"

Thrym smiled. "But good luck trying to get it back, for I have buried it eight leagues beneath the earth in a place that no one, god or man, can find."

"What reason do you have to steal the thunder god's most prized possession?" Loki demanded.

"I wish to make a deal," Thrym offered as an explanation. "I will return Mjölnir in exchange for the goddess Freyja's hand in marriage."

Surprised, but with no other solution, Loki took to the sky once more and returned to Asgard with the news. There he informed Thor of Thrym's demands, and the two men approached the goddess for a second time that day.

"Get your bridal veil ready Freyja, for today you shall marry Thrym, king of ogres." Thor announced.

"What are you blabbering about? I have no interest in marrying Thrym," Freyja scoffed.

"Well, it is the only way I shall get my hammer back, so you must." Thor crossed his arms with an air of finality, as if this explanation settled everything.

"You are ludicrous!" Freyja cried. "To come in here and demand I marry a man in exchange for a lump of wood and metal. To not even ask me if I would agree to your plan, like I am an object to be traded. Well, Thor, you would have received the same answer either way, but now I won't be nice about it. Get your hammer yourself! I lent you my cloak because I felt sorry for your predicament, but here is where I draw the line. I shall never marry a man I do not want to marry, least of all for the sake of a fool like you. My answer is no."

Heimdall, the watchman of Asgard, had overheard this conversation and decided to offer up an alternative solution.

"Thor," he began, "why don't you disguise yourself as Freyja and go in the goddess's place?"

"And make a fool of myself?" Thor scowled. "Why should I do such a thing when Freyja is right here?"

"Oh, be quiet," Loki interrupted. "Freyja has given you her answer, so if you want your hammer back, you'll have to do as Heimdall has suggested."

Thor stomped his feet and crossed his arms, scowling at the three figures before him. But none of them would budge. It was Freyja's right to refuse Thrym's hand in marriage, no matter what the god of thunder might desire. And so the goddess brought Thor a bridal veil to hide his face and lent him the golden necklace known as Brísingamen, which all the gods recognized as hers. Finally, after donning a wedding dress that covered him from neck to toe, Thor was ready to play the part.

With Loki disguised as his maid, they traveled to the giants' kingdom, and Thor presented himself as Thrym's bride. The new arrivals were welcomed by the ogre king and a feast was arranged in honor of the impending event. As they dined, Thrym clapped his hands and called out across the dining hall.

"Have the wedding gift brought out," he declared.

On the king's command another ogre stepped forward, holding in his hands the hammer Mjölnir itself. Gently, the king's servant placed the weapon in Thor's lap, none the wiser to who really lay behind the veil. What happened next occurred so quickly the king had no time to react. For, reunited with his hammer, Thor leapt from his seat and tore the wedding veil from his face. Without pause for thought, the god brought Mjölnir down on Thrym's royal head. And this was how Thor regained his hammer, and Freyja established her boundaries.

BE MORE LIKE FREYJA

While you might feel that you need to always help someone else with their troubles, you should never have to do anything you are uncomfortable with. Like Freyja, you can lend a helping hand without compromising your own safety or happiness. You'll find that throughout life there are numerous situations where it is important to set clear boundaries, first with yourself and then with other people. It might not even be obvious at first where to draw the line. But if you take your time, without allowing others to pressure you into something you're not ready for, you will often figure out where you stand by listening to your instincts.

No one else can set your boundaries; it's about what's right for you. And if someone tries to push you, remember that one small but powerful word wielded by Freyja: no. All of us, mortal or otherwise, are allowed to put our foot down when our boundaries are broken, and we should respect the boundaries of others too.

ADVOCATE FOR YOURSELF LIKE ASDZĄĄ NÁDLEEHÉ

NAME: ASDZĄĄ NÁDLEEHÉ

ALSO KNOWN AS ESTSANATLEHI OR CHANGING WOMAN

Do you find it hard to put your wants and needs before others?

Follow Asdzą́ą́ Nádleehé's example and put yourself first.

WHO IS ASDZĄ́Ą́ NÁDLEEHÉ?

Asdzą́ą́ Nádleehé is one of the central deities in the Navajo creation story known as Diné Bahane', which means "story of the people." The Navajo people make up one of the two largest Indigenous tribes in the USA alongside the Cherokee, and the Navajoland reservation is situated along the borders of New Mexico, Arizona and Utah. According to the Diné Bahane', Asdzą́ą́ Nádleehé was discovered upon a mountain by First Man when she was just a baby. First Man took the child home, and he and his partner, First Woman, raised her as their own daughter.

ASDŹÁÁ NÁDLEEHÉ'S STORY

A time came when Asdźáá Nádleehé had already lived a long and happy life. She had borne two brave warrior sons to Jóhonaa'éí, the Sun, and raised them all by herself.

When the twins were old enough, they set out from home to slay the monsters that plagued their land. First, they needed weapons, and so they sought the assistance of their father. From the Sun, the two men received a myriad of weapons, and it wasn't long before their enemies were defeated. Finally, when the world was at peace once more, they returned their arsenal to their father, who had one last message for them.

"Tell your mother to meet me atop the Giant Spruce Mountain in five days' time," Jóhonaa'éí said, "I want to create a home with her."

The two sons agreed and, returning home, they passed the Sun's message on to their mother, who was curious as to what Jóhonaa'éí might have to say. Five days later, Asdzáá Nádleehé seated herself upon a rock at the peak of Big Spruce Mountain, the same place where she had first met the Sun many years ago. As she reminisced, Asdzáá Nádleehé felt the weight of another body sit down beside her. She turned and locked eyes with Jóhonaa'éí for the first time in many years. Before she could speak, the god had put his arm around her shoulders, a grin spreading across his face.

"That's enough of that," she growled, returning his arm to him. "What is it you want?"

"I wish to be with you, Asdzáá Nádleehé, forever," Jóhonaa'éí answered. "To take you with me and make a home for us both in the west."

"I can't say I want the same," Asdzáá Nádleehé replied.

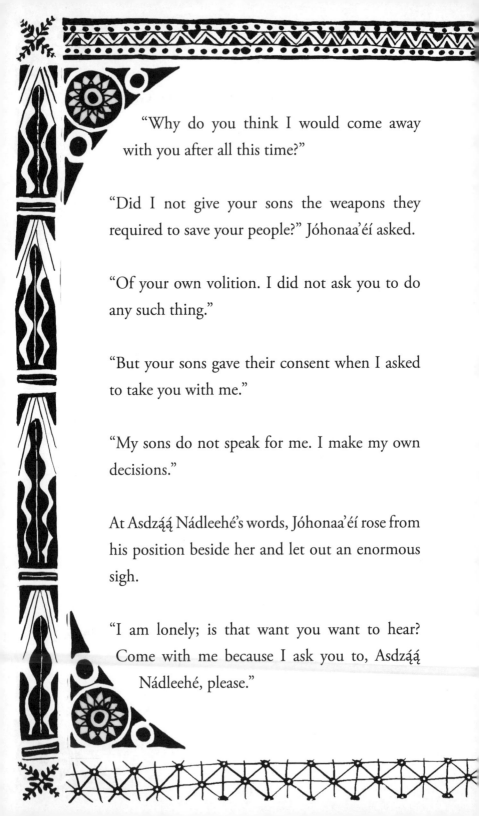

"Why do you think I would come away with you after all this time?"

"Did I not give your sons the weapons they required to save your people?" Jóhonaa'éí asked.

"Of your own volition. I did not ask you to do any such thing."

"But your sons gave their consent when I asked to take you with me."

"My sons do not speak for me. I make my own decisions."

At Asdzáá Nádleehé's words, Jóhonaa'éí rose from his position beside her and let out an enormous sigh.

"I am lonely; is that want you want to hear? Come with me because I ask you to, Asdzáá Nádleehé, please."

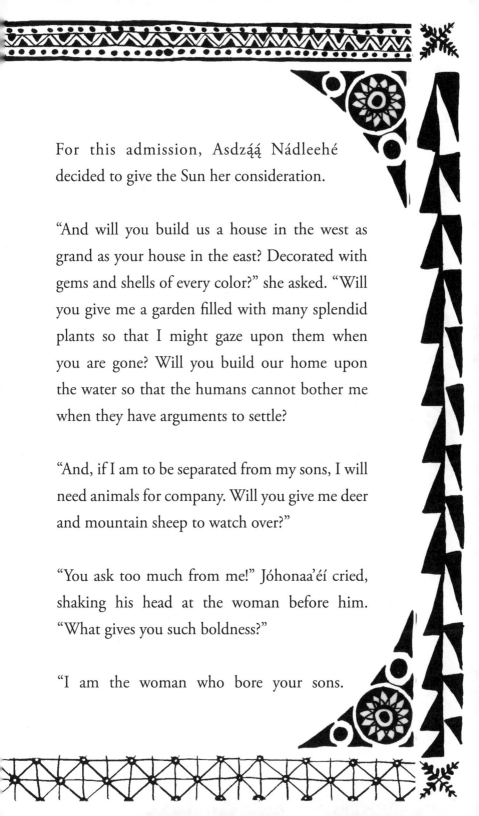

For this admission, Asdzą́ą́ Nádleehé decided to give the Sun her consideration.

"And will you build us a house in the west as grand as your house in the east? Decorated with gems and shells of every color?" she asked. "Will you give me a garden filled with many splendid plants so that I might gaze upon them when you are gone? Will you build our home upon the water so that the humans cannot bother me when they have arguments to settle?

"And, if I am to be separated from my sons, I will need animals for company. Will you give me deer and mountain sheep to watch over?"

"You ask too much from me!" Jóhonaa'éí cried, shaking his head at the woman before him. "What gives you such boldness?"

"I am the woman who bore your sons.

I endured pain you will never know to bring your children into this world. I protected them when they were young and too fragile to fend for themselves. I sacrificed my life to raise them to be brave and decent men," Asdzą́ą́ Nádleehé responded, her voice never wavering. "While our journeys may be different, Jóhonaa'éí, I am your equal. My needs are just as important as yours, and there will be no harmony between us unless you can learn that now."

At first, Jóhonaa'éí was silent, simply gazing down at the passionate and confident woman before him. Then, with great care, he returned to his seat and wrapped his arm around Asdzą́ą́ Nádleehé's shoulder once more.

"Of course, you are right. You shall have everything you ask for and more." He nodded.

"Then I believe we shall get along just fine," Asdzą́ą́ Nádleehé agreed.

BE MORE LIKE
ASDZÁÁ NÁDLEEHÉ

While it might come easy to us to champion a friend or family member's interests, we can often forget to fight for our own. Next time you find yourself in a position where you need to champion yourself, remember Asdzáá Nádleehé's story. Not once did she underestimate her worth. Instead, she spoke clearly and directly of what she expected from Jóhonaa'éí, making it clear that their life together was to be founded on equality between the two.

So remember, like Asdzáá Nádleehé, to recognize your own accomplishments and contributions, your needs and desires, and next time the opportunity arises, shout them from the rooftops until you're hoarse in the throat.

Advocate for yourself, because you deserve to be heard and valued.

SHARE WHAT YOU KNOW LIKE MAMA OCLLO

NAME: MAMA OCLLO
ALSO KNOWN AS MAMA UQLLU OR COYA
(MEANING "QUEEN" IN QUECHUA)

Do you want to find a way to help people, but just don't know how? Mama Ocllo might help you appreciate how much you can offer by sharing the knowledge you already have.

WHO IS MAMA OCLLO?

Mama Ocllo is the mother goddess of the ancient Inca people, an empire that stretched across North and South America between the thirteenth and sixteenth centuries. She was the daughter of Inti, the sun god, and Mama Quilla, the moon goddess. They sent Mama Ocllo and her brother, Manco Capác, down to earth to teach humanity the ways of the world. According to Inca tradition, the rulers of the empire were believed to be the direct descendants of Mama Ocllo and Manco Capác, as they were the first to reign over the Inca people.

MAMA OCLLO'S STORY

According to Inca legend, when humans first lived on earth, they did not know how to care for themselves. They had no houses or clothing because they didn't have the skills to make them. They scrambled for food because they did not know how to grow or store it. And they were angry and violent towards one another while in the pressure of survival mode.

The Sun and Moon watched the humans live like this for some time until they finally took pity on them. They turned to their daughter, Mama Ocllo, and their son, Manco Capác, and instructed them to take knowledge to the people down below. Once they had agreed, the Sun guided his two children to Lake Titicaca, where he left them to begin their journey. The two deities were on their own, trusted to guide humanity into a new age with only one instruction from their father. Before he left, the Sun had given Mama Ocllo and Manco Capác a single golden rod. This rod would tell them where they should build their first city for the humans to live. All they had to do was push the rod down into the earth, and if it could be completely covered, this meant the land was fertile enough to farm and grow.

So Mama Ocllo and Manco Capác set out northward together, for it seemed as good a direction as any. Along their travels they experimented with the rod, pushing it into the earth at various intervals. But no matter how many times they tried, they could never find soil deep enough for the rod to disappear. They carried on until they reached the Valley of Cuzco, a cold and desolate land. Despite appearances, the siblings tried once more to bury the golden rod, and to their dismay it sank into the ground with barely a thrust. They turned to each other with disappointment.

"We have finally found the land on which our city shall be built," Manco Capác said. "Perhaps it is time for us to part and head in two directions? That way we can both bring back as many humans as we can find."

Mama Ocllo agreed, and the two deities parted ways. Mama Ocllo headed south, and as she traveled, she encountered many men and women. Each time, she paused and sat with them, reciting the story of how her father, the Sun, had sent her to earth along with her brother. She told them of the city they would build together and how she would teach them to cultivate the land and grow food. Every human she encountered was encouraged by Mama Ocllo's vision, and so she sent them to the valley she had recently departed before carrying on her search for more souls in need. Finally, when there was no one left behind, Mama Ocllo returned to Cuzco, where her brother and the humans awaited her arrival.

First, Mama Ocllo and Manco Capác showed the humans how to sow and till the earth, creating fields where they could grow plants and vegetation for food. Then, they demonstrated how to build homes from stones and dirt so they would have somewhere dry to sleep at night. Steadily the city grew, and the land was divided into two, Upper

and Lower Cuzco. The former housed those brought by Manco Capác while the latter was home to those who had followed Mama Ocllo to the city. Both halves were treated equally, and the residents lived in harmony.

But the work of the god and goddess was not complete. Mama Ocllo continued the humans' education by showing them how to spin and weave. This way, they would be able to make clothes for themselves and their children, which would keep them warm when it was cold and protect their skin when it was hot. Meanwhile, Manco Capác showed the humans how to irrigate their fields so they would flourish, even beneath the pounding sun. And this was how Mama Ocllo and Manco Capác showed the people of earth a better way of life, through imparting the knowledge that they had to share.

BE MORE LIKE MAMA OCLLO

In everyday life, it can be easy to take what you know for granted. Whether it's something you learned a long time ago or something you practice on a regular basis, your knowledge and skills could be beneficial to someone else if you take the time to pass them on. You don't need to possess life-changing skills like growing food as Mama Ocllo does (although I'd love some tips on gardening if you have them). You might be great at budgeting or know which local cafés have vegan options on the menu. You might simply understand something a friend is struggling with.

Like Mama Ocllo guiding the first humans on earth, it is important to be generous with your knowledge and skills, no matter how big or small. Never underestimate the value of what you know, because what you pass on might end up changing someone else's life for the better.

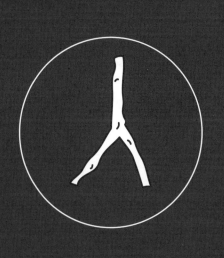

SHOW KINDNESS LIKE LEUTOGI

NAME: LEUTOGI
ALSO KNOWN AS LEUTOGITUPA'ITEA

Ever been made to feel like your compassion makes you an outsider? Leutogi's story might help you remember whose opinion really matters.

WHO IS LEUTOGI?

Leutogi is the Polynesian goddess of bats, originally from the island of Samoa. She began life as a human princess and the second wife of the Tongan king. During her mortal life, she was ridiculed for caring for an injured bat, the only species of terrestrial mammal native to the Polynesian islands. But when she was sentenced to death by her husband, it was the bats who saved her life, and so she became known as the goddess of bats.

LEUTOGI'S STORY

One warm afternoon, the princess Leutogi was wandering the island of Tonga where she was to marry its ruler, King Tuitoga. She was exploring her new home with one of the king's servants when she came across an injured fruit bat whose wing was trapped beneath a rock. The tiny creature was no bigger than her hand and covered in soft, dark fur. Bending down, Leutogi made to reach for the trembling creature, but the king's servant put out his arm.

"Stop; don't touch it," he demanded. "Bats are unnatural creatures, only good for food. Better it dies than live."

Leutogi did not care for the servant's words. The creature she saw before her was frail and hurt, and she would not leave it there to die. Pushing aside the

servant's arm, she gently removed the rock
from the bat's damaged wing and carefully picked
the animal up from the ground. Wrapping a banana
tree leaf around its body, Leutogi cradled the bat to her
chest while the servant ranted beside her.

"No true Tongan would touch such a disgusting
creature," he sneered, but Leutogi paid him no heed.

Leutogi had no doubt that the servant would tell
everyone what she had done, but she did not care. Of
course, the man did just that, starting with the king's
first wife, who already hated the young woman her
husband had decided to marry. Meanwhile, Leutogi
took the small bat into her hut, feeding and caring for
it as best she could. Whenever she left her home, the
other villagers whispered and laughed, mocking her for
her softness. She was ignored at meals, but this simply
made it easier for her to sneak small pieces of mango
and papaya away to feed to her tiny guest.

After a few weeks had passed, the bat had recovered
enough to fly on his own, and Leutogi released him
back into the wild. Before he left, she told the

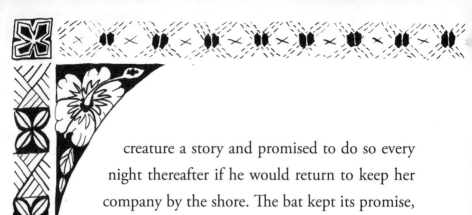

creature a story and promised to do so every night thereafter if he would return to keep her company by the shore. The bat kept its promise, and each night, Leutogi would regale him with tales of the Samoan people, and each evening, he would bring with him more of his kind so that soon dozens of bats visited her.

Meanwhile, during the day, Leutogi was tasked with assisting the king's first wife and her child. But there came a night when Leutogi was returning home and heard screams and shouts carrying from the queen's hut. Running towards the noise, she found a crowd had gathered inside the building. Leutogi pushed past the other figures and found a shaking finger pointed directly at her face.

"It's her fault!" the queen cried. "It's her fault the king's son is dead."

Leutogi didn't have a chance to find out what had happened before she was dragged away and sentenced to death by the king. The villagers tied her to a tree and stacked piles of wood at her feet. Leutogi would burn, they cried, before setting the wood alight. Leutogi did not know what else to do. She began to chant, her voice carrying over the crowds until it reached her furry friends. Almost immediately, swarms of bats began to circle overhead, releasing all the liquid in their bladders until the flames were quenched.

Furious, the king decided Leutogi would have to die another way. He sent the princess across the sea to a desolate island where nothing grew, and no one could survive. Each day, he would send one of his servants to check on Leutogi, hoping she was dead. But every time, the servant found Leutogi well fed and rested, waving to him happily from her seemingly barren rock.

"Where are you getting food, demoness?" the servant finally cried.

Leutogi smiled in answer and raised her hands to the sky. Countless bats swirled overhead with fresh guavas and mangos in their claws. Horrified, the servant grabbed the oars of his boat and rowed away as fast as he could from the strange woman and her pets. Leutogi did not mind; the bats were all the company she needed. They brought her food and she told them stories, including one of a woman who had saved an injured bat and found a friend for life.

BE MORE LIKE LEUTOGI

Sometimes being kind is easy and doesn't come with any negative consequences, but there are also times when being kind goes against the grain. You may even feel pressure to not be kind to someone if everyone else is ignoring them or being cruel, but when these circumstances arise, it's useful to consider if those acting unkindly are really the type of people you want to follow. Being kind might mean sacrificing relationships with people who can't respect the things you care about but, remember, if Leutogi hadn't ignored the opinions of the villagers, the little bat would have died, and she never would have known his friendship. Leutogi's bravery isn't loud or brash, it is determined and calm, prioritizing the wellbeing of another creature over her own reputation.

This legendary princess considered what she valued most, and it was kindness above all else. It may not have made her popular at home, but it counted to those who really mattered, those who stuck by her when times were tough and came to her aid when no one else would.

ACCEPT HELP
LIKE PSYCHE

—— NAME: PSYCHE ——

*Are you feeling overwhelmed
by a task that lies ahead?*

*Psyche reminds us that you don't
have to do everything alone.*

WHO IS PSYCHE?

Psyche was the Roman goddess of the soul, her name literally translating to "soul" or "breath" in ancient Greek. Little is known of her significance to ancient Roman religion, but her story has been preserved within a Latin novel by the writer Apuleius (who lived during the second century CE), known either as *Metamorphoses* or *The Golden Ass*. According to this tale, Psyche started out life as a mortal woman who married the god of love, Cupid. So that the couple might never be parted, Jupiter, the king of the gods, gave Psyche a cup of ambrosia, otherwise known as the food of the gods. Psyche drank the liquid and was made immortal, becoming a goddess in her own right.

PSYCHE'S STORY

There once lived a young woman named Psyche whose loveliness was so renowned that people would come from all four corners of the world to simply gaze upon her. They brought her gifts and bowed down before her as though she were a goddess and not a mortal woman. Venus, goddess of love and beauty, was forced to watch as her followers abandoned her shrines and temples, flocking instead to the kingdom where Psyche lived.

"How dare these mortals worship her instead," the goddess cried. Furious, she called for her son, Cupid, whose reputation for mischief proceeded him. "Go to Psyche and make her fall for a man so worthless she will regret the day she was first called beautiful."

Meanwhile, Psyche hated how men flocked to see her only to leer at her like an object. She wished dearly she could find a man who truly loved her. Psyche's father saw how miserable his daughter was, and so he traveled to the oracle at Delphi. Here he was told that Psyche must be sent away to the nearby cliffs, and there she would meet her husband. For he was no mortal man, but a creature feared by the gods themselves. And so the king and queen delivered their daughter to the cliff's edge and left her to her fate.

As daylight faded on the mountain, Psyche found herself transported to an enchanting glen. She could not believe her eyes. While the glen itself was magnificent, it held at its center an enormous golden palace befitting of a god. Upon entering the palace, Psyche was greeted by the voice of a man, but she could not see him anywhere.

"Welcome to your new home, my wife," he said. "While you can never look upon my face, know I will be a good husband to you. You must be weary. Retire to our chambers and once you have extinguished every light, I will join you there."

This was how Psyche's new life began. That night, in the darkness, her new husband joined her, and they whiled away the hours in conversation. Each night thereafter was the same. Psyche's husband would join her only in the pitch-black and they would spend their evenings in each other's arms. Slowly but surely, over the course of their time together, Psyche realized she had fallen in love with her faceless husband.

As happy as she was, Psyche still missed her family, and so one day she asked her husband if her sisters could be allowed to visit, to which he agreed. Upon their arrival she greeted them with a smile. Psyche's sisters were not happy to see her, although they hid it well. Here she was, living in a golden palace with a man she loved, while their own marriages were cold and miserable.

"Surely you must see your husband's face?" one asked.

"I promised him I would not."

"But have you not heard? A terrible monster plagues the countryside!" the second sister exclaimed. "And after all, it was foretold your husband would be feared by the gods themselves. They must be one and the same."

Psyche was shocked by this revelation, but little did she know it was simply a jealous lie.

"You must look upon your husband while he sleeps and find out the truth," the first sister insisted. "We will never sleep peacefully until we are sure you are safe."

That night, once her sisters had left, Psyche drew a candle from under her pillow and went to light it from a fire outside the room. Silently she leaned over her husband's sleeping form and held the flame aloft. What she saw took her by complete surprise. The man who lay beside her was more beautiful than any being she had ever seen. It was the god Cupid himself. Forgetting herself, she leaned in closer and a small drop of wax fell on to Cupid's arm.

With a start, the god opened his eyes to see his wife peering at him in the light. Before Psyche could say a thing, the god had flown from the room and out of their palace. Injured by both the candle wax and her betrayal, he collapsed alone beside a river, too distraught to do anything else. Venus soon learned of her son's deceit. The impudent boy had married the very girl she had ordered him to punish. Finding him by the river, she locked him away where he could never reach his wife, and then sent her servants to bring Psyche before her.

"You think you are a worthy wife for a god?" Venus shrieked at the terrified Psyche. "Let's see how worthy you are." The goddess ordered thousands of seeds and lentils to be poured on the ground at Psyche's feet.

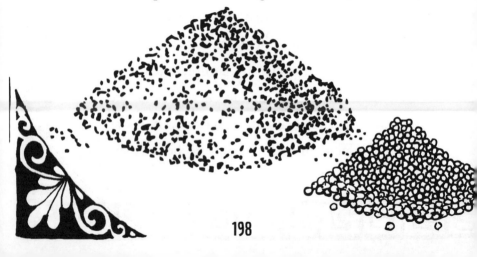

"Sort each of the grains before you into separate piles before nightfall."

Left alone to her task, Psyche buried her head in her knees and sobbed till her throat was dry. There was no way on earth she could possibly sort the stacks of grains in time. Little did she know there was a witness to her grief. A tiny ant had scurried by and, taking pity on the woman, gathered the rest of his family to aid her in her chore. Together the ants made short work of Venus's task, neatly organizing each grain into its own category before the sun had even begun to set. When Venus returned, she was furious.

"You cannot have completed this task alone," she screamed. "Well, if you are so clever, try this instead. See out there, over that stream, there is a herd of golden sheep. Fetch me some of their wool."

With that, Psyche was pushed towards the stream, but before she could cross the water, a small voice piped up from the reeds along the bank.

"Watch out, Psyche, those sheep are deadly! Wait until they fall asleep, and then you will be able to sheer their wool."

Psyche knew good advice when she heard it, and she heeded the kindly reed. Waiting patiently until the golden beasts had closed their eyes, she clambered across the stream and carefully detached fistfuls of their wool. When the young woman presented Venus with her prize, the goddess flew into another rage.

"You've been getting help; I know it! Let's see you try this. Journey to the mountain there and fetch a jar of water from the stream that feeds the wailing river."

Off Psyche went again, only to quickly discover what was so dangerous about this task. The stream was bordered on both sides by enormous dragons whose teeth glinted in the sunlight. What now, she thought, no longer even able to cry. At that moment she felt the tell-tale flutter of feathers by her ear as something heavy landed upon her shoulder: an eagle.

"Here, give me your jar," he offered, holding out one claw.

Not sure what else to do, Psyche did as the bird instructed, and off he flew. Soaring over the dragons' heads to reach the stream, he stretched out his leg and skimmed the jar along the water's surface until it was full to the brim. Once she had thanked the eagle profusely, Psyche returned to Venus's palace only to be met with fury once more.

"I have one last task for you, sneaky Psyche. Take this box to the underworld and ask the goddess Proserpine to place inside it a little of her beauty, just enough to last a day."

Psyche knew Venus's intent. In order to visit the underworld, she would have to die and never come back. Yet, seeing no other way, she took herself to the top of the highest tower in the goddess's palace with the intention of throwing herself from its height. Before she could jump, however, the tower spoke aloud.

"You need not die to complete your task, poor Psyche. If you journey to the city of Taenarus, then you will come across the ventilation holes to the underworld itself."

So Psyche followed the tower's directions and found the spot she was looking for. Climbing down through one of the holes, she traveled a long and winding path until she reached the palace of Pluto. Upon entering the grand hall, Psyche kneeled at Proserpine's feet and told her Venus's demands. The goddess was sympathetic to Psyche's plight and decided to help her. She took the box, but instead of doing as Venus had asked, she secretly placed inside a little trick for Venus. What Proserpine had not planned on, however, was Psyche opening the box herself. Back in the world above, Psyche grew nervous she might have failed her task, so the young woman lifted the container's lid to check inside. Without warning, she fell to the ground, sound asleep. Meanwhile, Cupid's wound had healed, and with a little effort, he had managed to escape his mother's clutches. Hearing of how Venus had plagued his poor wife, he was desperate to return to her. Cupid searched far and wide until finally he found Psyche's slumbering form. Brushing the cloud of sleep from her brow, he took her in his arms.

"You have returned," she gasped, returning his embrace.

"And this time I will never let you go."

Cupid was true to his words. For that same day, he took Psyche to Olympus with him where he presented her to Jupiter, king of the gods. Together, the two men presented the young woman with a cup of sweet ambrosia, which she brought to her lips and drank in full. Before their eyes, Psyche transformed, no longer a human woman but an immortal deity just like Cupid himself.

BE MORE LIKE PSYCHE

Hopefully no one is asking you to shear a flock of vicious, carnivorous sheep, but if they were, I would hope you'd accept any assistance offered. Whether it's because we don't have the time or knowledge to get the job done by ourselves, we all need a little help sometimes. Accepting help from others doesn't diminish your own abilities or contribution; it's simply admitting that some tasks are just too big to accomplish alone. And that's OK!

So, next time someone offers up a helping hand when you're in need, take it. As Psyche learned from the kindness of others, you don't have to struggle alone. But remember, sometimes it might be difficult for others to see when you need help, especially if you are one of those people who always seem to have it under control. If this is this case, then don't be disheartened when help isn't offered up straight away, because all you need to do is ask.

TRUST YOUR FEELINGS
LIKE MA

NAMES: MA
ALSO KNOWN AS NINAVANHU-MA

Has anyone ever dismissed your emotions or suggested you simply stop feeling them?

Consider channeling a little bit of Ma's confidence next time they do.

WHO IS MA?

Ma is the first goddess and the creator of the world according to the Bantu people of Africa. The Bantu people include more than four hundred different cultural groups across the African continent, such as the Zulu people of South Africa and the Baganda people of Uganda. After Ma created the world, she was joined on earth by the Tree of Life, with whom she conceived the first generation of humankind. When those first people, led by Za-Ha-Rrellel, betrayed her, she let all but one woman die. To this woman Ma gave the last of the Bjaauni, creatures created by Za-Ha-Rrellel, and bid them conceive the second generation of humankind: the Bantu.

MA'S
STORY

In the beginning there raged a never-ending war between cold and fire, both fighting for dominance, unable to find balance. The Great Spirit, uNkulunkulu, grew weary of their warring and so, from the ashes of their battle, he bade the first goddess create herself. Her skin was made of silver and her eyes of gold. She was of gigantic stature with four breasts, each topped with a nipple made of emerald. Her name was Ma. The first thing uNkulunkulu did when Ma was born was instruct her to create a world using the wasteful energy that cold and fire's war expended.

First, Ma created the stars, the sun included, using the sparks that fire left behind. Next, she formed the earth with all its hills and valleys from the same substance. Once this task was completed, Ma took a seat upon the highest mountaintop and awaited uNkulunkulu's next instructions. As she looked around, she was pleased with her work, but she could not help feeling as though some part of her existence was incomplete. It was lonely work to build a universe by herself, and uNkulunkulu was so far beyond her that his presence made no difference to her solitude.

While Ma waited atop the mountain, the feeling of isolation only grew. Overwhelmed, she began to weep. Her tears fell fast and heavy, so copious that they slipped down her cheeks and fell to the land below. Where the earth dipped and bowed, the water made its home, forming the rivers and lakes that had not previously existed. uNkulunkulu witnessed Ma's sorrow, but he could not understand her loneliness.

"Cease with this useless display of emotions," he commanded, his voice causing the earth itself to shake. "It is time to get up and carry on your work once more." Ma, however, was not so easily dismissed.

"Useless, you say? My feelings are not useless to me. What is the point in the stars if they just stare silently down at me? What is the point in this earth that cannot

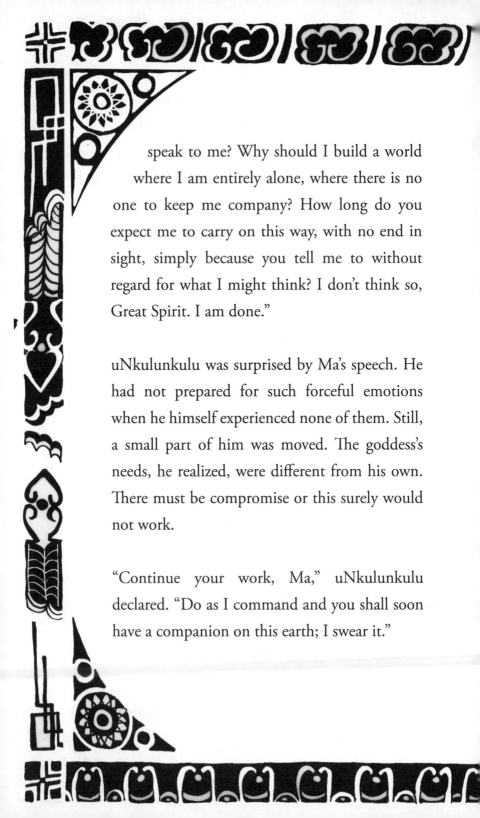

speak to me? Why should I build a world where I am entirely alone, where there is no one to keep me company? How long do you expect me to carry on this way, with no end in sight, simply because you tell me to without regard for what I might think? I don't think so, Great Spirit. I am done."

uNkulunkulu was surprised by Ma's speech. He had not prepared for such forceful emotions when he himself experienced none of them. Still, a small part of him was moved. The goddess's needs, he realized, were different from his own. There must be compromise or this surely would not work.

"Continue your work, Ma," uNkulunkulu declared. "Do as I command and you shall soon have a companion on this earth; I swear it."

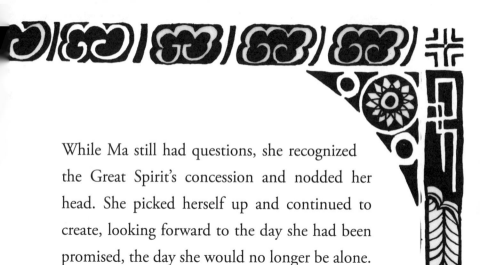

While Ma still had questions, she recognized the Great Spirit's concession and nodded her head. She picked herself up and continued to create, looking forward to the day she had been promised, the day she would no longer be alone.

BE MORE LIKE MA

Look, I won't pretend that everything is smooth-sailing for Ma from this point on. She goes on to face numerous trials throughout her story—trials that include being kidnapped by the very humans she brought into the world! But when I think of Ma, I think of the moment when she boldly claims her own feelings and insists on their validity.

There will come times in all of our lives where others question our emotions. They might dismiss our anger or sadness or imply we're irrational. We might even do this to ourselves. But we feel the way we do for a reason. Our emotions exist to tell us something, and no one else can decide how their words make us feel.

You don't have to overlook something supposedly 'small' if it offends or upsets you. You don't have to pretend someone's actions don't make you uncomfortable. Nor should you tell others to simply get over whatever they're feeling. Recognize and stand strong in your own emotions, just as Ma did when loneliness overwhelmed her.

LIVE
LIKE A
GODDESS

Wow, that was a lot to cover—from goddesses to life lessons! The thing is, there are still so many more incredible and inspiring goddesses out there, not to mention lessons to learn. The tales in this book might even have taught you something that I didn't think of when writing them down. The possibilities are endless, after all. But, in the meantime, if just one of the stories in this book helped you feel better able to face the world today, then I'm counting that as a success. Maybe next time you feel sad, you'll remember Brigid or the Sun. Or else when you need a little confidence boost, you might try channeling a little of Artemis or Freyja.

Remember, you don't have to be an all-powerful being to be strong and confident. You don't have to create the world to care about it or find your place in it. You don't have to know magic to possess valuable skills or knowledge. You don't have to be worshipped to be worthy of respect. You don't have to be a goddess to live like one!

RESOURCES

Below is a selection of resources you might fight useful if you have been affected by some of the issues covered in this book. Please note, many of these resources are specific to the UK and Ireland, but there are likely similar services available where you are, so do search online or ask your local medical provider.

ADVICE AND HELP WHEN FACED WITH DOMESTIC VIOLENCE

US

National Domestic Violence Hotline:

https://www.thehotline.org/

Child Help:

https://www.childhelphotline.org/

The Network/La Red:

https://www.tnlr.org/en/24-hour-hotline/

Abused Women's Aid in Crisis, Inc.:

https://awaic.org/getting-help/

Peaceful Families Project:

https://www.peacefulfamilies.org/dvdirectory.html

UK

Refuge: nationaldahelpline.org.uk

The Children's Society—Domestic Abuse:
childrenssociety.org.uk/information/young-people/advice/
domestic-abuse

Galop: galop.org.uk/get-help/

Women's Aid Survivor's Handbook: womensaid.org.
uk/information-support/the-survivors-handbook/

Barnardos: barnardos.ie/our-services/work-with-families/
childhood-domestic-violence-abuse/

The Muslim Women's Resource Centre:
mwrc.org.uk/what-we-do/helpline

ENGLAND

Women's Aid: womensaid.org.uk/information-support/

SCOTLAND

**Scotland's Domestic Abuse and Forced Marriage
Helpline:** sdafmh.org.uk/en/

NORTHERN IRELAND

Domestic and Sexual Abuse Helpline: dsahelpline.org

IRELAND
Women's Aid: womensaid.ie/help

WALES
Live Fear Free Helpline: gov.wales/live-fear-free

GRIEF COUNSELING AND OTHER MENTAL HEALTH SERVICES

UK
Child Bereavement UK: childbereavementuk.org

Cruse Bereavement Support: cruse.org.uk/get-support/helpline

NHS: nhs.uk/mental-health/talking-therapies-medicine-treatments/talking-therapies-and-counselling/nhs-talking-therapies/

Mind: mind.org.uk/information-support/helplines

Let's Talk About Loss: letstalkaboutloss.org/about

Grief Encounter: griefencounter.org.uk

Young Minds: youngminds.org.uk

Childline—Child and Adolescent Mental Health Services: childline.org.uk/info-advice/your-feelings/mental-health/child-adolescent-mental-health-services/

BIBLIOGRAPHY

American Indian Myths and Legends, ed. by Richard Erdoes and Alfonso Oritz

Black Rainbow: Legends of the Incas and myths of ancient Peru, collected by John Bierhorst

Cath Maige Tuired, anonymous, tr. from the Old Irish by Elizabeth A. Gray

Diné Bahane': The Navajo Creation Story, tr. from the Navajo by Paul G. Zolbrod

Hawaiian Legends of Volcanoes, ed. by William Drake Westervelt

Hawaiian Mythology by Martha Warren Beckwith

Hymn to Artemis by Callimachus, tr. from the ancient Greek by A. W. Mair

Indaba, My Children: African Tribal History, Legends, Customs and Religious Beliefs by Vusamazulu Credo Mutwa

Invisible Powers of the Metaphysical World: A Peep into the World of Witches by Yemi Elebuibon

Moralia: Isis and Osiris by Plutarch, tr. from the ancient Greek by Frank Cole Babbit

Legends of Maui, A Demi-God of Polynesia and His Mother Hina, collected by W. D. Westervelt

Metamorphoses by Apuleius, tr. from the Latin by Robert Graves

Orishas, Goddesses, and Voodoo Queens: The Divine Feminine in the African Religious Traditions by Lilith Dorsey

Pacific Island Legends: Tales from Micronesia, Melanesia, Polynesia, and Australia, ed. by Bo Flood, Beret E. Strong and William Flood

Shahnameh by Abolqasem Ferdowsi, tr. from the Persian by Dick Davis

The Devīmāhātmyam, anonymous, tr. from the Sanskrit by Devadatta Kālī

The Elder Edda, anonymous, tr. from the Old Norse by Andy Orchard

The Homeric Hymns: Hymn to Demeter, anonymous, tr. from the ancient Greek by Michael Crudden

The Huainanzi by Liu An, tr. from the Chinese by John S. Major et al.

The Mabinogion, anonymous, tr. from the Middle Welsh by Sioned Davies

The Nihongi: Chronicles of Japan from the Earliest Times to A.D. 697 by Yasumaro no O, tr. from the Japanese by William George Aston

The Origin of Tārā Tantra by Jo Nang Tāranātha, tr. from the Tibetan by D. Templeman

The Penguin Book of Mermaids, ed. by Christina Bacchilega and Marie Alohalani Brown

Yijarni: True Stories from Gurindji Country, ed. by Erika Charola and Felicity Meakins

ACKNOWLEDGEMENTS

I am indebted to all of the writers, mythographers, storytellers and historians whose work preserves the memory of the women that feature in this book.

I would also like to acknowledge my editor Helen Archer and the wonderful team at Wren & Rook for all of their hard work on *Live Like a Goddess*, as well as give special thanks to Nozomi Tolworthy for her input and Taylor Dolan for her beautiful illustrations.

Finally, a massive thank you to everyone who has ever helped me on my own journey through life, whether it be through their example, a conversation or writing their own thoughts down on paper; this book wouldn't exist without you.